THE GHOST NEXT DOOR
A Love Story

Ginny Baird

THE GHOST NEXT DOOR
A Love Story

Published by
Winter Wedding Press

Copyright © 2013
Ginny Baird
Trade Paperback
ISBN 978-0-9895892-2-2

Edited by Linda Ingmanson
Cover by Dar Albert

About the Author

From the time that she could talk, romance author Ginny Baird was making up stories, much to the delight—and consternation—of her family and friends. By grade school, she'd turned that inclination into a talent, whereby her teacher allowed her to write and produce plays rather than write boring book reports. Ginny continued writing throughout college, where she contributed articles to her literary campus weekly, then later pursued a career managing international projects with the US State Department.

Ginny has held an assortment of jobs, including school teacher, freelance fashion model, and greeting card writer, and has published more than twenty works of fiction and optioned ten screenplays. She has additionally published short stories, nonfiction and poetry, and admits to being a true romantic at heart.

Ginny is a *New York Times* and *USA Today* Bestselling Author of several books, including novellas in her Holiday Brides Series. She's a member of Romance Writers of America (RWA), the RWA Published Authors Network (PAN), and Virginia Romance Writers (VRW).

When she's not writing, Ginny enjoys cooking, biking, and spending time with her family in Tidewater, Virginia. She loves hearing from her readers and welcomes visitors to her website at http://www.ginnybairdromance.com.

Books by Ginny Baird

Holiday Brides Series
The Christmas Catch
The Holiday Bride
Mistletoe in Maine
Beach Blanket Santa
Baby, Be Mine

Summer Grooms Series
Must-Have Husband
My Lucky Groom
The Wedding Wish
The Getaway Groom

Romantic Ghost Stories
The Ghost Next Door (A Love Story)
The Light at the End of the Road
The House at Homecoming Cove

Romantic Comedy
Real Romance
The Sometime Bride
Santa Fe Fortune
How to Marry a Matador
Counterfeit Cowboy
The Calendar Brides
My Best Friend's Bride

Bundles
The Holiday Brides Collection (Books 1–4)
A Summer Grooms Selection (Books 1–3)
Real Romance and The Sometime Bride (Gemini Edition)
Santa Fe Fortune and How to Marry a Matador (Gemini Edition)
Wedding Bells Bundle

Short Stories
The Right Medicine (Short Story and Novel Sampler)
Special Delivery (A Valentine's Short Story)

Ginny Baird's

THE GHOST NEXT DOOR
A Love Story

Chapter One

Elizabeth set her hand on her hip and gazed out over the countryside. She and Claire stood by their silver SUV, parked at the top of the steep gravel drive.

"Thought you said it had a view."

She glanced at the fifteen-year-old girl beside her with long, brown hair and bangs. Dark eyes brimmed with dramatic expression.

"Jeez, Mom. You didn't say it was of a graveyard."

"Cemetery."

"What?"

"Graveyards are beside a church. Cemeteries are stand-alone—"

Claire's jaw dropped in disbelief. "If you're such a stickler for words, why didn't you read the fine print?"

"What fine print?"

"The one saying we'd be moving next to a haunted house?"

Elizabeth's gaze traveled to the run-down Victorian less than a stone's throw from the modern, prefab house they'd rented. She figured the land the newer house stood on had once belonged to the larger home, which now sat with murky windows, sunshine reflecting off of beveled glass. Its wide front porch was caked with dust, gnarly vines tangling their way around paint-cracked spindles holding the porch railings.

Elizabeth chided herself for not investigating further when the ad said *Bucolic, small-town setting. Unobstructed mountain views.* She hadn't known those views would be peppered with tombstones, or that they'd be living beside an empty house.

"Maybe it won't be so bad?" she offered hopefully.

A sharp wind blew, sending the twin rockers on the Victorian's front porch sighing as they heaved to and fro as if tipped by some unseen hand.

Claire frowned, turning away. "It's creepy. This whole place is creepy. I don't think we should stay."

A tension in Elizabeth's gut told her perhaps Claire was right. Even the rocking chairs tilting in the wind seemed a bad omen. But a greater tension in her wallet said she'd already signed a lease for the next nine months. There'd be no backing out of it without losing her security deposit plus the first month's rent.

Elizabeth drew a breath, studying the more positive parts of the landscape. The two-story place they'd rented appeared almost new, with a cheery front garden and a covered stoop. Its clapboard siding and slate roof were well kept, giving the home a cottagey feel. And the large side yard housed a sturdy oak, its leaves shimmering orangey gold in the October sun. "The setting may be a little unusual," she told her daughter, "but at least it's quiet."

"Yeah. Dead quiet."

"Come on," Elizabeth urged. "Help me get the groceries in the house. Then we can grab our luggage. We'll be settled in no time." She flashed the girl a grin. "Spaghetti for dinner."

Claire shrugged and reluctantly reached into the hatchback for some bags. "Whatever."

Later that night, as she and Claire stood drying dishes by the sink, Elizabeth questioned her wisdom in bringing them here. This rental property was pretty isolated, at least five miles from the tiny village nearby. But when she'd been searching for a temporary place for them to stay, there hadn't been a lot of options. Blayton, Virginia was so small it wasn't even on most maps. Set up against the Blue Ridge Mountains, it had once been an old railroad town, the gateway community between here and Tennessee on the far side of those high peaks. After a period of anonymity, it was now undergoing a minor renaissance, with a new microbrewery moving in, a few swank restaurants, and a burgeoning host of surrounding vineyards and upscale B&Bs. Though trains no longer stopped here, the working tracks remained intact, with the original station now converted into the local library.

Elizabeth had been sent here to revamp the old town newspaper, previously called the *Gazette*. Her larger news organization was intent on acquiring antiquated or defunct town papers and bringing their newer incarnations into the twenty-first century. Elizabeth had fought this relocation, begging her boss in Richmond to let her tackle this from afar. After all, the real focus of all their newer editions was virtual subscriptions offered on the Internet. But Jerry had argued she needed to be on the scene, get up close and personal with the local community to make this transition work. Besides, he persisted, in order for the new publication to be successful, it needed to develop *ground legs* too. Perhaps a younger readership might emerge online, but for the old-timers to get roped in, there had to be a physical edition of the paper as well. Something folks could pick up at the local grocery, which was extra convenient since there was only one store in town.

"Mom, look!" Claire's eyes went wide as the dish she was drying slipped from her hands. It collided with the linoleum at her feet and split in two.

Elizabeth stepped toward her daughter. "Honey, what's wrong?"

"Did… Did you see it?" Claire stammered.

She followed Claire's gaze out the kitchen window to the house across the way. Evening shadows shrouded the Victorian, its windows dark and dreary.

"Up there." She pointed to a window on the second floor. "I saw something move inside."

Elizabeth wrapped her arm around Claire's shoulder, thinking the day was getting to her. It had been a five-hour drive from Richmond, then there'd been unpacking to do. It was unnerving to be a teen and move far from your school and long-term friends. It had to be doubly upsetting to find your new home situated across the street from a cemetery. The poor kid was tired and overwrought, letting her imagination get the best of her. And Claire had quite an imagination. She'd taken first prize in her district's teen short-story contest and had recently turned her storytelling ability into songwriting while she plucked out accompanying music on her secondhand guitar.

"I'm sure it was nothing," Elizabeth told her. "Maybe just a shadow from the big oak outside."

Claire narrowed her eyes in thought. "Yeah, maybe." She bent to grab the broken dish, and Elizabeth stooped to help her.

"Here, let me get this. Why don't you go grab the broom and dustpan from over there in the corner?"

After the two of them had cleaned up, they once more stood by the sink and stared out the window.

"I'm sure it was just a shadow," Elizabeth said.

"You're probably right."

Just then a beam of light swept through the big house's downstairs, and Claire leapt into Elizabeth's arms. "*Mo-om!*"

Elizabeth held her tightly. "Hang on, I'm sure it's just a—"

"A *what*?" Elizabeth's pulse raced. "You said the house was empty! For sale!"

"Maybe it's a potential buyer?" Elizabeth said lamely, not for a second believing that was true. Who on earth visited creepy old houses as night fell? Maybe someone who worked during the day and couldn't get here otherwise, Elizabeth told herself logically. Just look at her, gripping her daughter like she was some freaked-out kid herself. Elizabeth knew better than that.

"Is it gone?" Claire asked, her eyes tightly shut.

Elizabeth returned her gaze to the window and the looming house next door. There wasn't a hint of movement anywhere. "No signs of life."

Claire popped both eyes open. "I wish you hadn't said that."

Just then the doorbell rang with a spooky twang, and Elizabeth yelped.

"Ow, Mom! What are you doing? It's just the front door."

Elizabeth released her grasp, feeling foolish. "Of course it is," she replied in an even tone. But they weren't expecting company and were miles from anywhere.

The doorbell chimed again, and Claire strode in that direction.

"Where are you going?"

"To answer it."

"Wait." Elizabeth protectively stepped in front of her. "Better let me." She was fairly sure ghosts didn't ring doorbells. But it certainly couldn't be a neighbor bringing cookies.

Nathan Thorpe stood on the stoop of the cozy house, holding a brimming plate wrapped in tinfoil. Walnut-chocolate chip. His specialty. He'd heard the new people had moved in and wanted to welcome them to town. Blayton didn't get many visitors. Full-fledged transplants were even rarer. Nathan couldn't recall the last time a new family had moved here. Might have been the Wilcutts when they bought the old mill store and converted it to a pool hall/saloon.

The door opened just a crack, and Nathan noticed the chain had been latched. A pretty face peered out at him. From his limited point of view, she appeared to be in her thirties and have captivating dark eyes. At least one of them.

"Can I help you?" she asked in a big-city voice that sounded very sophisticated. She also seemed a little skittish, like she wasn't used to living outside of suburbia. Could be the solitude was getting to her. But if that was the case after just one day, this poor lady was in for a long haul.

He smiled warmly. "Just thought I'd stop by and welcome you to Blayton."

She surveyed his khaki-colored uniform along with the gun in his holster. "You're the sheriff?"

He extended his plate. "Nathan Thorpe. Nice to meet you."

"Since when do cops bring cookies?" a girl asked over the woman's shoulder.

She turned and whispered back to a shorter person Nathan took to be her daughter. "I don't know."

Now there were two dark eyes in the door crack, one of them belonging to a face that was younger. Boy, city folk were weird. He'd nearly forgotten that part.

"Uh," Nathan began uncertainly, hedging his way back toward the stairs. "I can just leave these on the steps."

"Wait! Don't go." The door slammed shut, and he heard the chain slide off. A split second later, it opened again, and a stunning brunette greeted him. She was petite and wore jeans and a long-sleeved T-shirt. The teenage daughter beside her was dressed in a similar way, but her jeans were torn. Nathan gathered this was the fashion, and not that the girl had fallen and scraped her knees. He'd seen other kids dress like this as well. *Thrift-store chic,* his niece called it. "I'm so sorry. I… We…didn't mean to be rude. It's just that we weren't expecting anybody."

"Perfectly fine. I understand." He reached in his wallet and flipped open his credentials. "If it makes you feel any better, this proves I'm the real McCoy." He handed them over, still holding the cookie plate in his left hand.

"I can take that," the girl offered helpfully. Though he surmised it was because she'd caught a whiff of chocolate chips. Nathan's cookies had taken first prize at the county fair for three years running. Not that he ever bragged on himself. Other people did it for him.

Nathan passed her the cookies as the mom flipped shut his credentials and returned them. "I apologize for giving you a hard time." She had a youthful face, but those tell-tale crinkles around her eyes said she'd spent a lot of time worrying. Nathan knew it must be hard raising a girl on her own. The high school secretary said there hadn't even been a father's name listed on the matriculation form. He set his jaw in sympathy for this family, knowing that deadbeat dads weren't just a big-city ailment. Sadly, they were commonplace everywhere.

"I don't blame you for being cautious," he said kindly. "In fact, caution's often a good thing."

"Especially at three-way stops," the girl cut in.

"Exactly." His eyes twinkled and Elizabeth couldn't help but notice their shade, a heady mixture of blue and brown with just a hint of green around the irises. An unusual blend of color complemented by his uniform and tawny brown hair. He appeared to be about her age and was incredibly handsome, solid across the chest with a lean, athletic build. He tipped his hat toward Claire. "Nice to see we've got another good driver in town. I've got my hands full with the bad ones."

"Oh no, I don't—"

"She doesn't drive yet," Elizabeth rushed in, her words overlapping with Claire's. She smiled sweetly at her daughter. "But the time's coming soon."

"I'm sure she'll do fine." He shot each a cordial smile.

"I'm sorry," the woman said politely. "I'm Elizabeth Jennings. And this is my daughter, Claire."

"Pleasure," he said with a nod. "I didn't mean to keep you. Just wanted to let you know that I'm here, if you ever need anything."

Elizabeth's gaze inadvertently traveled to his left hand. At least, she thought her gaze was inadvertent. Surely she wasn't checking for a ring. Although she couldn't help but notice, there wasn't one. Not even a tan line left from where one might have been.

"How will we reach you?" Elizabeth asked.

He shot her a grin and her old-enough-to-know-better heart fluttered.

"Dial 9-1-1."

"Isn't that for emergencies?"

His brow rose in a pleased expression. "Will you be calling me otherwise?"

Elizabeth's cheeks flamed. "I meant, just in case it's something minor. A question, maybe."

He cocked his chin to the side. "9-1-1 will do. We don't get many true emergencies. Martha won't mind."

"Martha?"

"She mans the phones and for the most part spends her days extremely bored. I'm sure she'd welcome the chance to chat with you."

Elizabeth eyed him uncertainly. "Well, all right, if you're sure."

"Wouldn't be opposed myself," he muttered, turning away.

Elizabeth leaned out the door. "What's that?"

His neck colored slightly as he set his eyes on hers. "I said, call any time. No question is too big or too small."

"Ask him, Mom," her daughter urged.

"Do you know anything about the house next door?"

"The old Fenton place?" he asked, intrigued. "I know everything about it. Why?"

"We thought we saw someone in there," Claire said.

"Or something," Elizabeth added quickly. "Of course, it could have just been some shadows."

"What about the light?" Claire prodded with obvious concern.

"Light?"

"There was a sliver of something," Elizabeth said. "I don't know. It was too early for moonlight. I saw it too."

"Hmm." Nathan reached up and stroked his chin. "Could it have looked like this…?" He unhitched the flashlight from his belt and clicked it on, spreading broad beams across the stoop's floorboards.

Elizabeth swallowed hard. "You mean someone *was* in there? A person?"

Nathan appeared mildly amused. "Most certainly." He clicked off the flashlight, then clipped it back to his belt. "That was me."

"*You?*" Elizabeth and Claire asked in unison.

"Bob Robeson, the realtor, gave me a key. I stop by to check in once in a while. Ensure nothing is amiss."

Elizabeth felt her stomach churn. "Amiss how?"

"Nothing to trouble over," he answered. "Kid stuff. This time of year, especially. Sometimes teens play pranks. Dare each other to sneak inside and then spend the night. Nobody's ever made it, as far as I can tell."

"Is the place haunted?" Claire asked in all seriousness.

Nathan perused her kindly. "The house is old, sure. With a couple of strange legends attached. But haunted? Not likely."

Elizabeth was about to ask about those *strange legends* but stopped herself. Claire seemed on edge enough as it was. No need to go upsetting her child further with some idle, small-town lore. Besides, if Nathan assured them nothing was wrong, then what did the two of them have to worry about? He seemed an upright enough individual and was a man of the law besides.

"We appreciate you stopping by," she told him.

"And thanks for the cookies," Claire added.

"No problem, ladies. Enjoy the rest of your evening."

Then he walked down the path and cut across the neighbor's yard, heading to the drive around back.

"Where's his cruiser?" Claire asked.

"He probably parked it behind the house." She shut the door and locked it up tight, turning the dead bolt and sliding the chain in place for extra security.

"That was nice of him to bring cookies," Claire said.

"Yes," Elizabeth agreed. "Why don't we have a few with two cold glasses of milk?"

Later that night, Elizabeth walked to the window to draw the blinds as she prepared for bed. Across the country road abutting her house sat the empty graveyard. Moonlight glinted off tombstones as a hoot owl called. The window was up just a tad to let in the breeze and freshen the air.

Though this house couldn't be more than five years old, it smelled as musty and stale as an old cupboard. A floorboard creaked, and Elizabeth's heart pounded. Her gaze traveled to the side window facing the neighboring house. The rockers next door swayed gently in soft gusts of wind. *Now who's letting her imagination get the best of her?*

Elizabeth tugged shut the window, thinking she'd never sleep a wink hearing things go creak in the night. Suddenly, something caught her eye, and her blood ran cold. There, straight in her line of vision and at the highest point on the hill, sat two newly dug graves. It seemed impossible that she could have missed them before, mounds of fresh earth heaped high upon each, but she couldn't recall having seen them at all. Elizabeth scolded herself for being spooked by what was obviously a routine occurrence. Of course people were buried there. She just hadn't expected to take a daily head count.

Thank goodness their stay here was only temporary and that she wouldn't need to worry over their imperfect dwelling for too long. As soon as she was able, she'd investigate alternate lodging. In the meantime, she had other priorities. Claire started school on Monday, and Elizabeth had serious work to do. She had the key to the old newspaper shop and planned to make the place gleam like new.

Chapter Two

The next morning, Elizabeth surveyed the rundown corner shop that was to become her new work home. A worn wooden sign beside the weathered door read *The Town Gazette* in stenciled lettering. The front window was clouded over with cobwebs gathering on the inside. Through its murky pane, she spied an old wooden desk, swivel chair, and what appeared to be an ancient manual typewriter draped in a leather cover. Elizabeth wondered how long this paper had been out of commission. She thought her boss in Richmond said ten years. From the looks of this place, nothing had been happening in the Blayton periodical business for over a half century. She stared down at the key in her hand thinking she might as well let herself in and get busy straightening up. She just prayed it had modern conveniences like electricity and indoor plumbing. Wireless service would be nice too, but was probably too much to hope for. She'd need to call somebody local to have that installed.

"This place sure has seen better days."

Elizabeth peered over her shoulder to find Nathan standing there, sunlight bouncing off his hat. She couldn't help but notice it had warmed up quite a bit these past few days. It was only nine o'clock, and already she felt overheated in her sweater. "Nathan," she said with surprise. "It's great to see you."

"You too." He smiled. "Need any help opening up?"

"I'm assuming the key will turn in the lock."

He glanced past her and stared through the window. "I suppose I should have asked if you need help picking up. Not exactly tidy in there."

"I think it's mostly dust and cobwebs." She slid the key in the lock and jimmied it open to demonstrate. But when she pushed open the door, Elizabeth fell back with a gasp. "Oh," she said, choking on the word "Worse than I thought." Stale air hung heavy as dust assaulted her lungs.

Nathan followed her into the shop, covering his mouth with his sleeve. "I think we should open some windows." He pointed past the desk and typewriter. "There are a few more in back."

She nodded, and he strode across the room, heaving a couple of sashes skyward and sending a blast of autumn breezes into the room. "Keep the front door propped awhile," he told her. "That will help some of this clear out while we get to work."

"We?" Elizabeth asked in surprise.

"I can't let you handle this alone." He gave her a serious frown, but his hazel eyes twinkled. "Could get dangerous."

"Dangerous?"

"You could be attacked by dust bunnies."

Elizabeth burst out laughing. "That's really nice of you, but don't you have a beat to walk or something?"

"I'm on it." He patted the radio strapped to his belt. "Anything comes up, the dispatcher can reach me here."

Elizabeth didn't see how she could inconvenience him to help her on a cleaning mission. Then again, there were some awfully big newspaper bins in the corner she wasn't sure she could move by herself. "I'll tell you what," she said. "I'll let you help with the heavy lifting, but I'll do the cleaning. This is my"—she glanced around the room with a grimace—"place of business after all."

"It will be a great place," he assured her, "once it's all neatened up. And, it's got the best view in town."

"Oh?" Elizabeth followed his gaze out the dirty window and across the street to a quaint little coffee shop. Nestled right beside it hung a placard proudly stating *Town Sheriff.*

"Your office is right over there?"

"Yes, ma'am," he said, never taking his eyes off hers.

"Then I guess I'll always feel safe when I'm working."

"That's the general idea," he answered. "Helping the folks in Blayton feel safe."

But even as he said it, Elizabeth felt dangerously close to losing her way. For the past twelve years since Claire's dad had left, she'd resolutely steeled her heart against going astray. She had two important jobs to focus on. First, she needed to tend to Claire and provide stability, serving as both mother and father in the absence of a second parent. Next, she had to ensure there was always food on the table and a roof over their heads, because, if she failed at that, it wouldn't matter what kind of great mom she was. Without supplying life's basic needs, she'd be letting her daughter down. From time to time, Elizabeth had noticed an attractive man. She'd even spoken with a few and had gone out more than once for a cup of coffee. But the moment she'd been asked on a nighttime date, her heart backed down. She couldn't drag herself, much less her tender child, through another potentially traumatizing relationship. The stakes were simply too high.

"I'm sure you do a great job."

"I do what I can. Plus," he added, "I've got a good deputy to help me."

"I don't believe I've met the deputy."

"No, I suppose you haven't." He studied her thoughtfully. "In fact, I'll bet you've met almost nobody in town."

Elizabeth shook her head. "Apart from the school secretary and you." She glanced down at the bucket of cleaning supplies she'd toted in. "And, oh yeah, the nice lady at the Dollar Store where I bought all these. I believe she said her name was Jane?"

"Janet Campbell. Nice gal. Married to my deputy in fact."

He smiled warmly, and Elizabeth's breath caught in her throat. This time, she didn't believe it was from the dusty air. It was in the way he looked at her, and each time he did, he seemed to be looking deeper. Way down into her soul to the secret part of her that screamed, *I haven't had a boyfriend in forever and have almost forgotten how to converse with a very hot, single man!* "Really?" She was embarrassed to hear her voice come out as a squeak.

"Almost everyone in Blayton's connected somehow. You stay here long enough," he said with a wink, "you'll become connected to someone too."

It was impossible to tell if he was flirting or just being friendly. She'd been out of practice longer than she knew. "I'm hoping that Claire and I will make some friends."

"You've already got one." He adjusted his hat. "How did you like the cookies?"

Elizabeth's face warmed all over. "Oh gosh, I didn't thank you! I'm so sorry." She swallowed hard to stop herself from stammering like an idiot as he just stared down at her with an appraising smile. "They were delicious. Thanks. World's best chocolate chip. Not a one is left."

"It's good to know they were appreciated."

Elizabeth admitted to herself she'd appreciated more than the cookies. She'd been happy Nathan had stopped by and felt glad to have the chance to get to know him. With him headquartered right across the street, it might prove easy to get to know him better. Her foolish heart leapt at the possibility he might feel the same. "You don't really need to stay here and help... I'm sure you've got things to do."

"A few," he said with a grin. "But I don't mind moving some boxes first."

After he'd hauled some dusty old crates out back and shifted the furniture into position at Elizabeth's direction, Nathan folded his arms with a nod. "I think that just about does it." While he'd been working, she'd been busily dusting the room and mopping the old hardwood floors with oil soap. In no time at all, the place had been transformed from dreary into a space with actual potential. All she had left to do was clean the windows and go through the desk and filing cabinet drawers.

"It looks a thousand times better already," she proclaimed, leaning into her mop. "I've got to be honest. It *was* a little scary at first."

Nathan viewed her with understanding. "A lot of things seem scarier than they are. It appeared awful. Until you got to know it—one cobweb at a time."

Elizabeth laughed, enjoying his sense of humor. "I wish I could do something to repay you."

He replaced the hat he'd removed while he'd been working, and tipped it toward her. "All in a day's work."

"Will you come to dinner sometime?" she asked, blurting out the words the moment the thought had occurred and before its ramifications could form in her brain. A simple invitation to a meal didn't have to mean she was hitting on him. Did it?

She watched his neck deepen a shade behind the high rim of his collar, thinking maybe it did. "I'd like that," he answered. "Be very pleased to have dinner with you and Claire.

"But first," he said. "I think I should introduce you around. Help you get to know the town's folk a bit."

"That would be nice."

"How about you stop by the station when you finish up here? If you're not too tuckered out from cleaning, that is."

Elizabeth didn't believe her being overtired later seemed likely. Not when just looking in his eyes left her feeling energized. Almost like a teen girl on the verge of a… *Oh no, not that…* Elizabeth's heart skipped a beat. *A crush.*

Nathan headed back across the street to his office in a happy mood. Of all the strangers who'd come to Blayton since he'd been here, Elizabeth was by far the most interesting. Didn't hurt that she was very pretty besides. Her daughter seemed like a nice girl too. And nice teenagers were a bonus in this town. He thought of his niece, Melody, wishing she'd get her meanness under control. He knew it had to do with things at home. Nathan's sister, Belle, was a single mom doing her best with the girl. But her job at the library kept her busy afternoons and weekends, too. Melody was bitter over all the things she had to miss out on due to her mom's work schedule, and their tight family finances. She hadn't been able to participate in cheerleading or go on the class field trip. Nathan helped them out when he could, but the fact was he didn't make a ton of money. Then again, Nathan wasn't in his job for the money. He had bigger reasons for being the sheriff, most of them centered on setting things right. Everyone here had something they wanted, a goal they were working toward it seemed. At times they were aware of it, and at others they weren't. Like in Melody's case, where her duty was to grow into the caring young woman her family knew she had the ability to be.

Nathan made his way into the station and spotted Martha at the front desk, her nose in a book. The middle-aged woman with red hair and a round face glanced up with a pleasant smile. Her real job was manning the 9-1-1 line, but since it seldom rang, he never commented on her rabid reading habit. "Morning, Sherriff," she said, setting a bookmark in her book. Nathan noticed there was a stack of others by her coffee mug, several of which he'd offer to return to the library when he visited Belle later. "Can I get you some coffee?"

"Thanks, Martha, but I'm set for now."

And he was too. Just the thought that he'd be seeing Elizabeth later put an extra skip in his step and made him feel charged all over like he'd already had loads of caffeine.

"Morning, Nathan!" Bernie called from the back office. His deputy sat with his feet propped on his desk, working the morning crossword puzzle—from a decade ago. Since the *Gazette* had gone out of business, Bernie didn't have a regular paper to feed his addiction. So Belle had been kind enough to dig up a heap of out-of-print editions from the archive room at the library. She didn't mind getting rid of them, as they'd already been scanned and saved in electronic format and were headed to recycle anyway.

For Bernie's part, he was *pleased as punch* that he could engage in his favorite pastime and cheat when the need arose. More than once Nathan had caught Bernie sneaking a peek at the following week's paper to nab a word or two that had vexed him from the solution box. Though Bernie was barely pushing thirty, he often came out with real old-timey expressions that made him sound like he was more than twice that age. Nathan wasn't sure why, though he suspected it had to do with the number of years he'd spent in Blayton.

The pace of things was slower here, and everything a little retro. But still, when Nathan had arrived, the town felt right. It was a warm and welcoming town, and Nathan liked the people. Everyone was genuine, and genuinely concerned about each other. Except for a few outliers that were still coming along. Nathan sat at his desk, thinking of his niece, Melody. Eventually, she'd make progress too. Because as backward as Blayton seemed, folks here always tended to move forward—sooner or later.

Claire was just shutting her locker when two girls accosted her, one on either side. The first one was skinny and blonde with a boyish figure and cool blue eyes. "You're new here, aren't you?" she asked in a tone that wasn't quite friendly.

Claire glanced warily at the second girl, a shorter redhead, who stood nearby clutching her algebra book to her chest. "Today's my first day."

"That's what we thought," the smaller girl said. "My name's Joy."

"Yeah, yeah. And I'm Melody, but that's really beside the point."

Claire steadied herself on her heels, not sure what to expect. A warm welcome to Blayton High didn't appear in the offering. "What is the point?" she asked as evenly as she could.

Melody gave an exaggerated sigh. "You moved next to the Fenton place, didn't you?"

"I'm not sure I—"

"The creepy old house?" Joy filled in.

Mirth danced in Melody's eyes as she leaned forward. Claire instinctively wanted to inch back but held her ground. "You *did* hear it was haunted?"

"I don't believe in ghosts."

Melody and Joy exchanged glances, and a shiver raced down Claire's spine as if she'd been exposed to a chill.

"Then you're in for some fun," Melody said.

"Ghostly fun," Joy agreed.

"Thanks for the tip, but I was on my way to lunch."

Claire tried to step past them, but Melody blocked her path with her tall frame. "The lady who lived there was murdered, you know. In her sleep."

Joy solemnly nodded. "Nobody found her for weeks."

"Weeks and weeks." Melody lowered her voice in a vicious whisper. "And when they did... Her old tabby cat was eating up the corpse."

Joy assented with light brown eyes. "Poor thing was starving."

Claire's stomach clenched. Not so much at their ridiculous story as at the thought two ninth graders could be so cruel, purposely tormenting a newcomer. Not that she hadn't seen the same thing happen in her hometown. But there, it always happened to someone else. Claire was never on the receiving end. Nor on the side dishing it out. Claire simply didn't have it in her.

"What are you two up to now?" someone asked, approaching. Claire peered over Joy's shoulder to see a cute boy with dark brown hair and eyes moseying down the hall.

Melody turned with delight. "Perry! I didn't think you were here today?"

"Got in late," he answered, still walking forward. He gave Claire a lazy smile, the sort that turned up higher in one corner, and her heart did a tiny cartwheel. "Hello? And you are…?"

"I'm Claire," she said, relieved at last to see a friendly face.

"Nice to meet you, Claire. I'm sure Melody and Joy have been showing you the ropes?"

More like trying to trip me with them, Claire thought but didn't say. Instead, she answered, "We were just getting acquainted."

Melody narrowed her gaze at Claire in warning. As evil as she and her sidekick, Joy, were, Melody apparently didn't want Perry finding out. "We were just telling her how great it is having a new girl in our class," Melody lied.

When Perry glanced at Joy for confirmation, she added, "And welcoming her to the school."

Perry seemed to be weighing whether or not to believe this. "Well, now that your welcome is done, you probably have some place to be."

"Oh no, I don't think I—" Melody began.

"Don't you both have lunch detention?"

Joy's face grew long. "He's right, Mel. Maybe we'd better get going. Mr. Harris will tack on another day if we're late."

Perry shrugged at them like, *what can you do?*

Melody's face flushed pink.

"Catch you later," Perry said.

Both girls pursed their lips, hesitating. It was obvious they were reluctant to leave, especially Melody, who had barely taken her eyes off Perry since he'd gotten here.

He made an exaggerated display of pulling his cell from his pocket to check the time.

"Yeah, right," Melody finally said. "We'd better go."

"See ya," Joy added, addressing Perry before scooting off.

Perry's gaze trailed the pair as they traveled down the hall. "Hope they didn't give you trouble."

"Trouble?" Claire asked, feeling her own face flame.

His eyes fell on hers. "They're not the nicest duo at Blayton, if you know what I'm saying."

And boy, hadn't Claire experienced that firsthand. Still, she said, "Nothing I can't handle."

"You look like you can probably handle a lot."

"Hey!"

His lips crept up in a grin. "I meant that as a compliment."

Claire shifted on her feet, feeling her tensions ease. "Thanks."

Perry motioned to the brown bag she gripped in her hand. "What's for lunch?"

"Peanut butter and jelly."

"Can't go wrong with that."

"Nope."

"You got someone to eat with?"

Claire lowered her chin. "Not exactly."

"You do now," he said when she looked up. "I know a great spot in the sun. No one will bother us there."

"You mean it's far from lunch detention?"

Perry laughed. "Way far. Clear around the corner and on the other side of the building."

"Sounds very cool."

Perry led Claire around the big brick building to a back patio dotted with picnic tables. A few facing the football field were empty. He motioned for her to sit, and she slid onto a bench while he sat across from her. "So, how come you're in Blayton?" he asked, extracting a submarine sandwich from his bag and unwrapping it. It was loaded to the brim with all sorts of meats and cheeses, heaped with lettuce and tomatoes too. Claire stared down at her own sandwich, slightly envious. Of course, she had nobody to blame but herself. She'd insisted long ago that her mom give up on preparing her lunch. She was too old for that and could certainly slap some peanut butter and jelly on wheat bread herself. She took a bite, thinking it wasn't half bad, though not nearly as delicious as Perry's sub appeared.

"It was my mom's idea. Not *her* idea, really. Her boss's. To tell you the truth," Claire continued, "I don't think she wanted to come here any more than I did."

Perry stopped eating to look at her. "Blayton's not so bad, once you get used to it."

She studied his warm brown eyes. "How long have you been here?"

He appeared thoughtful a moment. "About three years."

"So you went to middle school at Kenan?"

He swigged from his water bottle. "And man, wasn't that wild."

"What do you mean?"

"Just that it was middle school, you know?"

She smiled like she did, but wasn't sure what he meant.

"Crazy kids doing crazy stuff." He shook his head. "And Melody and Joy? Believe it or not, they were arch enemies then."

"Really?" She leaned forward with interest. "What happened?"

"Melody started some kind of rumor about Joy that turned the rest of their girlfriends against her. By now, though, most of them have moved on."

"Moved away, you mean?"

"Yeah. That's how it is here. People come and go. More than you'd think for a small town."

Claire polished off the rest of her sandwich and started her apple, considering this. "Where did they go to? Those other girls?"

Perry shrugged. "Who knows? It's not like anybody ever tells us kids. Some mornings you just wake up and people are gone."

An unsettling tingle raced down Claire's spine. She dismissed it as a weird feeling she didn't understand. "I guess families move sometimes. Mine did."

He began chomping on some kettle chips. "Anyway, the point is, after that, neither Melody or Joy had too many friends left, so they decided to stick together. For better or worse."

"Seems like *for worse* to me."

"You nailed that one." Perry chuckled. "But don't let them get to you, all right? Joy's not so bad. And believe it or not, Melody has her good side."

"If you say so."

"Oh, it's there, I've seen it. She just doesn't like letting people know."

"Why not?"

"It's a power thing. She doesn't want to lose control."

"Of...?"

"Her standing in the school as most popular girl, reigning queen...and closet class bully."

"Wow."

"Yeah, but mostly I think she's afraid of herself."

To Claire's amazement, he opened some tinfoil, exposing a mouthwatering chocolate-chunk brownie. "I'm sorry if this is personal, but I've got to ask."

He met her eyes, and Claire heart rose in her throat. Perry was the cutest boy she'd ever seen. He was certainly the hottest guy she'd ever sat this close to.

"Ye-es?" he prodded with a grin.

Claire felt the perspiration build at her brow. "Who makes your lunch?"

"I do."

"*You?*"

"Well, okay, I'll be fair. My uncle made the brownies."

"You're pretty lucky to have an uncle like that."

"Don't I know it." He split the brownie in two. "Here," he said, handing her half. "I'll share."

Chapter Three

After eating her packed lunch, Elizabeth finished cleaning out the desk's drawers. Most of the paperwork was decades old, the majority of which could be discarded. She set aside anything that seemed important to ask Nathan about later. If he didn't know, maybe the town librarian would have an inkling regarding whether any of these old news notes held value. Elizabeth sighed and shut the last drawer, eyeing the covered typewriter on the desk. She'd saved its unveiling until the very end. Not knowing what she would find or the condition it might be in, she didn't want to ruin her hopeful anticipation.

Elizabeth was long past employing typewriters, and the only one she'd ever used had been electric. But still, the moment she lifted the worn leather cover, she knew she had a real gem in store. There it sat, the most perfect Royal Quiet DeLuxe, in pristine condition, keys gleaming like they'd been polished yesterday. It was a beauty, shiny, and black with stenciled gold lettering. She took a tentative strike at a key, and it clunked heavily against the cartridge, hitting with forceful precision. Elizabeth instinctively massaged her knuckle, thinking her fingers were nowhere near primed to take that sort of daily beating. Folks back then must have gotten used to it. Then again, they hadn't known any different. Laptop computers with easy-touch keypads were light years away when this was invented. She ran her hand across the top of the machine, thinking it would make a lovely office mascot. She might even position it with some other historic items, like original copies of the *Gazette,* in the front window. But that could wait until tomorrow. Today, she wanted to be home in time to meet Claire's bus. While she wouldn't precisely be standing on the corner—which would embarrass Claire no end—she did want to be there, perhaps with a fresh batch of goodies in the oven. Elizabeth knew this move was hard on Claire and understood the transition couldn't be easy. She wanted to do everything she could to help smooth things over. But first, she thought, checking the time with a smile, she had a date to keep.

Martha set down her book and stared at Nathan. "You expecting someone, Sheriff?"

"Not really," he said, pacing back toward his office.

Martha glanced down at the carpet and the invisible path he had worn. "Could have fooled me."

Nathan lifted the coffeepot and nonchalantly poured himself a cup. "What would drive you to say that?"

"Oh…just the fact that you've walked back and forth to the front window at least half a dozen times," she said in a lilting tone. "In the past ten minutes! Say, weren't you across the street earlier? Helping that newcomer out?"

Nathan took a sip of java, avoiding her gaze. "I was just being neighborly."

She got that smug little pout on her lips like she did when she thought she knew something. "You made her chocolate chip cookies, didn't you?"

"I make everyone cookies. Everyone new in town, that is."

"Not *everyone*, Nathan, and you know it."

He set his cup on the edge of her desk. "I do so. When the Wilcutts moved in, I took some to them."

"As I recall, that was lemon bars."

"And the Daniels family—"

"Strudel."

"State what you've got to say, Martha."

She met his gaze with an impish grin. "Just that your chocolate chip cookies spell L-O-V-E."

He squared his chin. "Come on."

"Took first place at the fair, didn't they? As I recall, the blue ribbon read *Most Likely Baked Goods by a Bachelor to Make a Woman Fall in—*"

"Hello?" The front door pushed open with a whoosh of air and its dangling bell chimed. Nathan's face fired hot as Elizabeth stared at him wide-eyed. "Oh good! It's you."

"Uh-huh," Martha clucked, shooting Nathan a glance.

"Elizabeth! Great." He cleared his throat, which had suddenly constricted. "You done cleaning up over there?"

She nodded, smiling at Martha. "I'm Elizabeth Jennings. We're new in town."

"So I've heard," Martha said, beaming. "Martha Holt." She extended her hand to shake Elizabeth's. "Nice to meet you."

"Same," Elizabeth said. She surveyed the small station with its old-timey radio on display. "Quaint. I've got something of that vintage over at my place."

"The typewriter?" Martha queried.

"That's the one. But how did you—?"

"Used to work with Pinkney Gale. He was the old news editor before you came. Naturally, that was some time ago."

"She probably guessed that from the cobwebs," Nathan added, settling his hat on his head. He turned to Elizabeth with a smile. "Ready to see the town?"

"As long as I'm home by four."

"That's when the high school gets out," Martha explained to Nathan, as if he didn't know. "My girl goes there too," she told Elizabeth.

"Really? That's great. Maybe she and Claire will be friends."

"Better chance of that than of Nathan's niece stepping in."

"Martha, please."

Elizabeth turned to Nathan as he led her toward the door. "Your niece?"

"It's a long story, but she's coming along."

"You kids coming back here after the tour?" Martha shouted after them.

Nathan pulled shut the door with a wink. "Don't count on it."

Once on the street, Elizabeth burst out laughing. "Oh my, that Martha's something! I mean, very nice, but—"

"Yeah," Nathan said. "She knows pretty much everything about everybody. So be careful what you tell her."

Elizabeth laughed again, liking it here. She'd never lived in a small town before. While it clearly was different from the larger metropolis she was used to, it held its own charm. As they turned toward town, Nathan halted suddenly. "Hang on. Would you mind waiting here a second? I forgot something."

"No problem," she said as he bolted back up the front steps to the station. He slipped through the door, then reappeared a moment later holding a stack of books.

"What are those?"

"Promised Martha I'd drop these by the library. We're stopping by there anyway."

Elizabeth eyed him with admiration, thinking that Nathan was the sort of guy who did nice things for everybody, even those who obviously razzed him. She didn't know what Martha had been teasing him about before she'd walked into the station, but Elizabeth had a heady intuition that it had a lot to do with her. Her and the fact that Nathan had offered to show her around. While it was a generous thing to do, Elizabeth suspected it wasn't a welcoming service Nathan provided to everybody. "It's nice of you to introduce me to people."

"I'm happy to do it."

"You really are some kind of sheriff."

He glanced at her, and his hazel eyes twinkled. "Am I?"

"A good kind, I mean."

"A bad kind wouldn't do."

"No."

"Elizabeth," he said, his gaze still on hers, "I'm awfully glad you moved to Blayton."

"Thanks. It's good to be here." And when she said it, the words rang true. Though she'd initially rejected the move and especially had protested it because of her daughter, something deep inside told Elizabeth this was where she and Claire were meant to be.

The next hour sped by in a blur of happy chatter and welcoming faces. They stopped by the Dollar Store and the corner market and met Bernie by the Dairy Queen, where he was filling the tank of his cruiser. But their first stop had been at the library, where Elizabeth met Nathan's sister Belle, the librarian, and he dropped off his haul of books. By the time they walked back to the newspaper shop where Elizabeth had parked, her feet ached and her tongue was all worn out from talking. She hadn't known they could cover so many miles in such a small area, or that she—normally an introvert—would find herself so suddenly extroverted among a passel of strangers. Something was different about Blayton. Elizabeth felt at ease and alive here. It was almost as if the whole rest of her life had been a dream, and she was just now—at age thirty-three—finally waking up.

She and Nathan stood on the sidewalk beside her SUV. "Thanks for taking me around today," she said. "That was special. Really made me feel…included."

"I'm glad." His smile warmed her through and through. "I hope you'll like it here."

She already did. Perhaps a tad too much. Her heart was already beating faster just because he was near. She opened the driver's door, and Nathan tilted his hat.

"Don't think I've forgotten."

"Forgotten?"

"About that dinner invitation."

Elizabeth's pulse pounded in her ears. "Yeah, right," she said, feeling her world flash hot, then cold, then warm again… "I'll call you."

"Just dial 9-1-1," he said with a grin.

When Claire walked in the door, Elizabeth was pulling warm banana bread from the oven. "So, how was school?"

"Okay."

"Just okay? Did you meet anyone?"

"A couple of kids." Claire set her backpack on a chair, then dropped down into another. "Smells good. What's cooking?"

"Banana bread. With pecans, just the way you like it."

Claire seemed mildly distracted. She pulled out her cell and began busily checking for messages. "The service here stinks."

"Cell service?"

"Yeah."

"I'm sorry, hon. These are probably old towers."

"I don't think they even *have* towers in this place."

Elizabeth turned the hot loaf onto a cooling rack. "Maybe not."

"Even at school, I got only one bar."

"You're not supposed to be using your phone at school."

"I was checking for messages from you," Claire said smoothly.

"Hmm, yes. Well, luckily I didn't call. I'll remember to phone through the office if I ever need to get in touch for some emergency."

Claire's gaze flitted to the landline. "When's the Wi-Fi going in?"

"Sometime this week, I hope."

"I was worried we'd have to do dial-up."

Elizabeth sputtered a laugh. "I don't think Blayton is *that* retro. Want a piece?" she asked, cutting a steaming slice.

"Sure, thanks." Claire rose to her feet. "I'll get the milk."

"So," Claire asked when they were both settled at the table. "How was your day in town?"

"Fine."

"Fine?"

"Yeah. I mean, great. Things went really well."

"Meet anyone?"

"Lots of folks! Nathan was nice enough to show me around."

Claire raised an eyebrow. "Sheriff Nathan?"

Elizabeth felt unnervingly as if she were under a microscope and that Claire could see right through her. At least straight down to her rapidly pounding heart. "What?"

Claire took a bite of bread. "I think Nathan likes you."

"What makes you say that?"

"I don't know. He looks at you funny."

"Funny how?"

Claire's lips broadened in a grin. "Like he thinks you're hot."

"I'm much too old to be hot."

"No, you're not."

Elizabeth's face warmed. "Thanks, honey. It's nice of you to think so."

"I'm not the only one…" Claire teased.

Elizabeth slapped her arm. "What makes you such an expert all of a sudden?"

"Life."

"Really?"

"And, maybe I met a boy at school."

"Claire!"

"A cool guy. A *friend*."

"Of course, that's what I thought." But from the stars in her daughter's eyes, Elizabeth believed Claire was interested in being more than *friends* with this boy. "What's his name?"

"Perry."

"That's a nice name."

"It's a name, Mom. Just a name."

"Right."

"So is Nathan."

"Argh!" Elizabeth leapt to her feet and hugged her girl. "I love you so much."

"I love you too."

"We're going to get through this, you know. This transition. Together."

"I know," Claire said, hugging her back.

Elizabeth awoke with a jolt to a wailing sound. What was that awful cry that sounded like a tortured soul in the night? She clutched the covers to her chest and blinked hard, trying to make out her hazy surroundings. The room came into focus, a haunting glow from a full moon streaking through the window. She'd been so whipped from her day, Elizabeth had forgotten to draw the blinds. She'd slipped into her pajamas in the bathroom, brushed her teeth, and hit the hay like an exhausted farmhand after a tough day. It couldn't have taken her more than five minutes to fall asleep, and her slumber had been deep. Miles deep, until this murky awakening… Something screeched again, its sound ravaging the darkness. Her bedroom door flew open, and Claire raced inside.

"Mom! Did you hear it?" Claire's face was ashen in the moonlight, panic registering in her eyes.

Elizabeth gathered her wits, trying to calm her daughter. "There has to be some logical—"

Reeeoowww! It hollered again, and Claire leapt onto her bed. "What is it?" Claire beseeched as Elizabeth wrapped her in her arms.

"I don't—"

There was the sound of glass breaking and a strange commotion in the house next door. Elizabeth and Claire tentatively rose from the bed, holding hands.

"It came from over there," Claire said, staring out the window. The ancient Victorian stood silent in haunting shadows. Claire squeezed her hand tight. Time was a vacuum as they watched and waited, hearing nothing more as the minutes stretched on.

"I'm calling Nathan," Elizabeth finally said.

"Good idea," Claire replied without loosening her grip.

Twenty minutes later, Nathan returned to their door with a flashlight. "I think I've found your ghost," he said, holding a large tabby cat in one arm.

"What?" Elizabeth asked in shock. For the ten minutes he'd been in there, she'd been a knot of nerves, not knowing what he might find. Not knowing if he'd get hurt. Fearing he might not return at all.

"You poor baby." Claire extended her arms toward the kitty, and Nathan passed him over. "Were you in there all alone?"

"He apparently got into some trouble," Nathan said. "Knocked a mirror off a dresser and broke it clear to pieces."

"That's bad luck," Elizabeth responded.

"Cats have nine lives," Nathan returned with a wry smile.

Elizabeth pondered the cat, now purring loudly in Claire's arms as she scratched him under the chin. "I don't understand. How did he get in there?"

"There's an old basement window that keeps coming loose. Critters crawl in from time to time."

"Some girls at school said old Mrs. Fenton had a cat."

"Don't let those urban legends scare you," Nathan said. "Nothing but nonsense."

"What urban legends?" Elizabeth wanted to know.

"I'll tell you later." Claire lifted the cat toward her chin, nuzzling him closer. "Can we keep him?"

She glanced at Nathan. "He's probably got a home."

"Might at that," Nathan said. "I'll ask around."

"In the meantime?" Claire pleaded.

The cat purred louder as if granting his assent.

"Only for the night," Elizabeth acquiesced. "Until Nathan checks around."

Claire's cheeks glowed bright pink. "Thanks, Mom!" Then she scurried off with the cat, presumably to pour him a bowl of milk.

"I want to thank you for coming by," Elizabeth said to Nathan when it was just the two of them. "I didn't know what to do. I mean, who else to call."

"You did the right thing," Nathan told her. "In fact, it made Martha's night. It's the second call she's gotten all month!"

"Who was the first one from?"

"Confidential. Police business."

"Of course."

"Though I can likely predict that third call."

"Oh?"

A slow grin spread across his handsome face. "It's coming from 312 Oak Street."

"But this is 312 Oak Street."

"Exactly," Nathan said, pinning her in place with his gaze.

Elizabeth felt her body warm from head to toe. "Why, Sheriff," she flirted, "are you angling to get asked to dinner again?"

"Might be."

"What's your Friday like?"

"I believe I could work in an opening. That is, if you don't mind my being on call."

"I suspect the sheriff is always on call."

"Yes, ma'am."

"Then, it's a date." The moment the words flew from her mouth, Elizabeth kicked herself a billion times. *A date? Elizabeth? Really?* "An engagement, I mean. An agreement to have supper."

Nathan tipped his hat with a smile. "If that means you're cooking, I accept."

A few nights later, Nathan sat across the kitchen table from his sister, Belle, and her girl, Melody, as they all ate sloppy joes. "Appreciate you having me over."

"We like having you over," Belle said with sincere blue eyes. "Besides…" She rolled her gaze toward her daughter. "You're a good influence around here."

Nathan set down his sandwich, picking up his sister's cue. "You behaving yourself at school?"

The girl's face fell, but she didn't answer.

"Melody got detention again."

Nathan addressed his niece, unable to mask his disappointment. "Oh, hon, really?"

"It wasn't my fault!"

"Don't go blaming Joy," Belle said sternly. "She told the principal that shaving creaming the girls' locker room was your idea."

"Easy for her to say."

Nathan evenly met her gaze. "You've got to stop getting yourself into mischief, Melody Anne. And start acting like a grown lady. You're practically sixteen now."

Melody huffed and dabbed her mouth with her napkin. "Can I be excused now?" she asked her mom.

Belle sternly addressed her child. "Your uncle's talking to you."

"Yeah? What's he gonna do? Throw me in jail?"

"Melody!" Belle tried to stop her daughter as she sprang from the table.

"It's all right," Nathan said softly. "Let her go."

"But I can't let her talk to you like that."

Nathan sadly shook his head, sorry for Belle and the trials Melody put her through. "I'll have a chat with her later."

After he'd helped Belle tidy the kitchen, Nathan rapped at Melody's door.

"Go away!" she yelled through it.

"You're not in trouble, if that's what you're thinking," Nathan called back.

He heard padded footfalls, then Melody's door cracked open. She stared at him with suspicion. "Why not?"

"Because I know you didn't mean to."

"The locker room?"

"Be disrespectful."

Melody heaved a sigh, and suddenly appeared fragile, like the angelic seven-year-old she used to be before her world went sour. "I'm sorry, Uncle Nathan."

"Everything passes, you know?"

"What do you mean?"

"The hard times, Melody Anne." He drew a breath, then released it. "I know it's not easy being fifteen. I was that age once myself. And I know it especially hasn't been easy on you…for a lot of reasons. But that doesn't mean you have to take it out on everyone else."

She hung her head, but he could tell she was listening.

"Your mom loves you a good deal. And listen up, kiddo. Your uncle here loves you too. You've got two great folks in your corner. That's more than a lot of people can say these days, you know."

She raised a hand to wipe her cheek, and Nathan suspected she was crying. "But why did he have to do it? Why?" When she raised her gaze to his, her eyes were bleary. "I begged him not to go, really I did. But he just picked up his suitcase and—"

Nathan pulled her into his arms as she broke down. "There, there," he said, gently patting her back. "I know."

She gripped him tightly, sobbing against his chest and Nathan's heart split in two. He didn't know how Belle's ex had been heartless enough to do it, but somehow he had. Up and walked out on his perfectly decent wife and child. None of them ever knew why. And nobody knew where he'd gone. Those were the sticking points. "But you listen up, little girl. There is one guy here who's never going to leave you, you hear?"

Tears streamed down her cheeks and her chin trembled. "Swear to God?"

"Cross my heart and hope to die."

Belle walked in, quickly surmising the scene and wrapped her arms around them. "We're family," she told them both, "and family sticks together."

Nathan held them tighter. "Yes, we do."

Later, on the front porch, Belle told him, "I want to thank you for that in there. It really helped. Having you around always helps."

"I'm glad to be here when I can. I just wish I could do more."

"You do plenty." She shared a weary smile. "You doing anything on Friday? They're having Harvest Night at the orchard, and I thought I'd take Melody."

Nathan knew Harvest Night was a good time, complete with hayrides and hot apple cider, but this Friday he had plans. "Love to, but some other time."

Belle curiously eyed her brother. "Got something else going on?"

"I might."

"Something involving that pretty brunette you introduced me to?"

"You women are so suspicious." But when he turned his back, Nathan's lips parted in a grin.

"I want to hear all about it!" Belle called after him.

He strolled off, breaking into a bright whistle.

"I'm serious! Saturday! Over coffee!"

Nathan held up a hand in a wave but kept on walking. Spilling to Belle after his night at Elizabeth's? Like that was going to happen. It wasn't such a big deal anyway. He was just going for dinner with the two of them, Elizabeth and Claire. It wasn't like he had a date. Not that he'd know what to do with one if he had it. Nathan mentally tried to calculate the last time he'd been out with an eligible woman. An eligible woman he felt attracted to, and who hadn't been one of Belle's or Martha's set-ups. But his mind grew foggy and he couldn't think that far back. Especially since all he was eager to do now was look ahead. The day after tomorrow, he'd be sitting down to supper with the Jennings. He didn't know why, but there was an unexpected lift in his heart just at the thought.

Chapter Four

By the time Friday came, Elizabeth was a ball of nerves. All she was making was chili, for heaven's sakes. Yet she'd already burned a batch of corn muffins and had nearly tossed the salad onto the floor.

"Want me to help with that?" Claire asked, watching her dump her burned disasters from the muffin tin into the waste bin. "I can make the next batch if you'd like."

Elizabeth tucked a strand of hair behind her ear. Claire helping out would be good. That would give her a few minutes to take a breather and freshen up before Nathan got here. "Do you mind?"

Claire warmly patted her back. "Nope. You go on upstairs and make yourself hot."

"Claire!"

"You're not telling me you haven't thought about what to wear?"

"Well, I…" Elizabeth glanced down at her cut-off shorts and T-shirt. It had been another warm, Indian-summer afternoon, and she'd become overheated working in the small kitchen. "Probably not this, right?"

"Probably not that," Claire agreed. "At least put on something not torn."

"These aren't torn! They're cut-offs!" Elizabeth set a hand on her hip. "Besides, you wear clothes with tears in them all the time."

"I'm fifteen."

"Point taken."

Phantom sauntered into the room and wrapped his way around Claire's legs. She'd named the cat the night they'd found him and didn't seem ready to lose him anytime soon.

From the cat's loud, humming purrs, the feeling was mutual.

"Looks like somebody's hungry," Elizabeth said as Claire bent down to stroke him.

"Yeah, this *somebody's* hungry all the time."

"Maybe trying to make up for being so skinny."

"Poor baby," Claire said, scooping him into her arms. "That right? Nobody used to feed you?"

She glanced at Elizabeth, who was turning to make her way upstairs. "You know what those mean girls said?"

"Which mean girls?"

"Melody and Joy at school."

"No."

"They said that Phantom here was old Mrs. Fenton's cat, come back from the wild after hiding out in the woods all this time."

"Well, maybe he is."

"They said he left because he ate her."

"What?"

"Mrs. Fenton."

"That's ridiculous."

"I know." Claire scratched Phantom under his chin, and he purred louder. "But do you think this is really her cat? The one she used to keep?"

"Mrs. Fenton? I don't know. Nathan said her cat ran off more than five years ago. That was before he came to Blayton, so he couldn't say for sure. He did ask around, though. Nobody in town seems to be missing a big, hungry tabby."

Just then the doorbell rang.

"Oh no!" Elizabeth cried as panicked gripped her. "What time is it?"

"Five till seven."

"I can't believe he's early!"

"Go on," Claire urged. "Run upstairs and change, and I'll let him in."

"But what about the muffins?"

"He can help," Claire said brightly.

Nathan stood on the front porch tapping his boot tip against a wooden board. It felt good to be out of his uniform and in a flannel shirt and jeans. Even if he was still on call, he didn't technically have to dress the part. Especially when the most likely emergency would be somebody's cat getting stuck up a tree.

He hoped he hadn't been overly presumptuous in bringing the apple cake. But, hey, if Elizabeth didn't want to serve it for dinner, she could save it for breakfast tomorrow. Nathan felt a tad guilty about finagling his way into an invitation. Then again, hadn't Elizabeth been the one to hint she'd ask him over initially?

He glanced over at the Fenton place, where two worn rockers creaked in the wind against darkened windows. They did lend the house a creepy air. Nathan would need to talk to Mr. Robeson about having them removed. He'd mentioned it to the realtor once before, but Robeson had insisted they gave the property a homey feel, *"real down-home country-like."* Now that Nathan was viewing the scene at twilight, he could understand why Elizabeth and Claire had been spooked about moving in next door. You couldn't find a more fitting poster child for a haunted house. Especially in October.

A sunny face appeared in the window glass beside the front door, then Claire pulled it open with a grin. "You baked for us again?"

Nathan pursed his lips a beat, hoping he hadn't made a misstep. "Apple cake. I hope you don't mind. I had an overabundance of apples."

"You get them from the Riley's?" she asked, letting him in.

"Their orchard, that's right."

Claire relieved him of the apple cake and led him toward the kitchen. For the life of him, Nathan thought he smelled something burning. "Mom will be happy you brought this. She loves apple everything!"

Nathan's face warmed, feeling he'd made a score. Claire was a good kid, and pretty mature for her age, from what he'd seen. "Maybe you know Perry? His uncle runs the orchard."

Her cheeks took on a pink hue. "He's in my grade at school."

"That's right. Along with my niece, Melody."

"Melody's your niece?" Claire asked with undisguised shock.

"I'm afraid so. And her friend Joy is my secretary's daughter."

"Small town." Claire peeled back the tinfoil wrapping the apple cake and took a whiff. "Mmm. We'll have to have this for dessert."

"Only if Elizabeth agrees."

"Agrees to what?" she asked from the threshold. Nathan turned to find Elizabeth standing at the entrance to the kitchen. She was prettier than ever, dressed in jeans and a light blue sweater to ward off the evening's chill. While the days here still heated up a bit, by nightfall they tended to cool down. Nathan was glad that fall was coming. Many folks greeted it with chagrin, feeling it marked the end of summer. But for Nathan fall was always full of possibilities: crisp air and new beginnings. This year in particular, it seemed things might finally change for him. And Nathan had waited forever for that change to come.

"Well, hello," he told her. "You look nice."

"Thanks, you too. I don't think I've ever seen you out of uniform."

"He brought us apple cake," Claire said happily.

"Did you now?" Elizabeth met Nathan's gaze, and he felt his heart go *ka-chunk*. "That was sweet."

"It was the least I could do," he told her. "Considering I practically asked myself over."

Elizabeth laughed, and it was like music to his ears. "Oh, I think I was aiming to ask you anyway."

Claire studied them a moment before asking, "Should I start the new muffins now?"

Nathan's brow rose.

Elizabeth blushed. "I kind of burned the first batch."

"No matter," he said breezily. "We can skip the bread if you'd like. We've got apple cake for dessert."

"Sounds like a great plan," Elizabeth said. "Truth is, I'm all cooked out."

And she was too. Even though all she'd done was follow the cooking instructions from the back of the chili mix, the entire ordeal of browning meat and mixing in beans had proved exhausting. Elizabeth didn't know why preparing this simple meal had taxed her so, beyond the fact that she'd hoped to make things perfect. It was hard not to hold that ambition with the perfect dinner guest coming over. Since the rest of the meal was ready and the table set in the next room, she invited Nathan and Claire to go ahead and start serving their salad and chili.

"Ladies first," Nathan insisted, stepping aside.

"But I'm the cook!" Elizabeth protested.

"All the more reason you should serve first and get off your feet sooner."

Elizabeth flushed at the fact that he could likely read her exhaustion. It wasn't as if she'd cooked a four-course meal, for heaven's sakes. Yet still, she felt a little lightheaded from her extended efforts. Or maybe it was having Nathan's gorgeous hazel eyes upon her that made her head swoon. He noted two empty wine goblets on the counter beside a bottle of red. "Want me to open this?"

"That would be great," Elizabeth answered, ladling chili into her bowl.

Claire subtly nudged her elbow. "Mom," she said in a hushed whisper.

Elizabeth studied her plate with a start, seeing she'd completely missed the bowl's lip and had been heaping chili onto the floor! Not that Phantom seemed to mind, as he coiled around her ankles and lapped at the mess by her feet. "Oh, no!"

Nathan quickly set down the wine and snatched some paper towels off a nearby holder, stooping to help her as Claire pulled Phantom out of the way. "Why don't you go take a load off while we clean up here?" Nathan told a mortified Elizabeth.

"Yeah, Mom. I can serve your chili."

"And I'll bring the wine!"

When Elizabeth slipped from the room, Nathan addressed Claire. "She always this nervous around dinner guests?"

Claire met his gaze with big dark eyes. "Not typically."

When Nathan had his first taste of chili, he saw it was true. Nobody could be a nervous Nelly in the kitchen full-time and yet learn to cook like this. "Great chili," he told Elizabeth, sampling another bite. "Is that a hint of cinnamon in there?"

"Just a dash," she answered proudly. Elizabeth seemed to have calmed down quite a bit since the kitchen mishap.

Perhaps the glass of merlot she was drinking helped. It sure assisted with Nathan's state of mind. Being here with these two gals felt real relaxed and homey. If he was the imagining sort—which he wasn't—Nathan could almost picture the three of them in some far-flung real estate ad Robeson concocted. *Get away from it all in Blayton. Laid-back country living and clean country air. The perfect respite for you and your family.*

Family? Nathan set down his wine with a jolt, the berry-colored liquid nearly splashing over the rim of the glass.

Elizabeth's pretty face creased with concern. "Everything all right?"

"Fine. Just fine. The whole meal was delicious."

Claire eagerly stood to clear their plates. "Can I serve the dessert?"

"That would be great, honey."

"Great kid you've got there," Nathan told Elizabeth once Claire had gone.

"Thanks. I'll keep her."

"Wish all teenagers were that easy to deal with."

"Claire has her moments, trust me."

"None that I've been able to spot so far."

"Would you like coffee with your apple cake?"

"I'd like that, thanks."

"If you'll excuse me a second, I'll go and put some on."

Elizabeth passed Claire in the kitchen as she headed to the dining room with dessert plates. "It's going good, Mom," Claire said in a low whisper.

"Stop it."

"I saw how he gazed at you when he nearly spilled his wine."

Elizabeth primly flipped back her hair. "And how was that?"

But Claire just shot her a cat-that-swallowed-the-canary grin and kept walking.

Elizabeth's pulse pounded in her ears as she filled the coffee canister with water. It was crazy for her to feel like a nervous teenager just because she was having some guy over for dinner. Some guy who'd been incredibly nice and welcoming to both her and her daughter. A guy who looked like sin in a uniform, and like someone Elizabeth wouldn't mind sinning with when he was out of it. Elizabeth swallowed hard, shocked at her raging thoughts. She couldn't actually want to…? She hadn't even kissed a man in over a decade and had long since given up on the idea of love. But when Nathan met her eyes, her insides went all marshmallowy.

She scooped grounds into the basket and switched on the coffeemaker, thinking she'd need to watch herself. Here she was, the new girl in town, and she had her daughter to think of besides. She couldn't go jumping headlong into some far-flung relationship with a man she barely knew. That would mess up everything. Yeah, right. Like her excellent life of solitude and lonely hearted existence. She could hear Claire and Nathan chatting easily in the next room and felt glad they were getting along. It was nice for Claire to visit with a man for a change. An adult man who was kind and seemed interested in what she had to say. Claire was young and already making friends at school. Soon Claire would be driving herself around and be out having fun more often than she stayed home. A few years after that, she'd be leaving for college, and Elizabeth would still be here—something whined at her feet, and she glanced down—with Phantom, forever angling for his next meal.

"Sorry, buddy," she told him, "no coffee for you." But she knew what he was really after: the creamer that Claire habitually snuck him when Elizabeth's back was turned.

They were just finishing up Nathan's superbly moist and tasty apple cake when the landline rang. "I'll get it!" Claire stood quickly and strode toward the kitchen.

"We don't seem to get very good cell reception out here," Elizabeth told Nathan.

He nodded in agreement. "I've heard they've planned some new towers, but I haven't seen any going in yet."

"Isn't that a problem for you? In your line of work, I mean?"

He thumbed the transistor at his belt. "Short-wave radio. Works like a charm. In any environment."

"Maybe I should get one of those to keep track of my daughter," Elizabeth joked.

As if on cue, Claire reappeared, a happy upturn to her lips. "Can I go to Harvest Night with Perry?"

"Tonight?" Elizabeth asked with surprise. "Isn't this a little sudden?"

"Teenagers are always so last minute," Nathan said with an informed smile.

"He only found out he'd have the night off just now," Claire said.

Nathan explained that Perry helped his Uncle Dan run the orchard. They had a big fall festival the first Friday of October. It was a huge town event and loads of fun.

Claire waited expectantly, her hand cupped over the mouthpiece of the handset. "*Puleeze?*"

Elizabeth glanced uncertainly at Nathan.

"He's a good kid," Nathan said. "I can vouch for him."

"How will you get there?" Elizabeth wanted to know.

"Perry's picking me up."

Elizabeth swallowed hard, not sure she was ready for this. "He's driving already?"

"He's got an early birthday," Nathan filled in. "But I wouldn't worry. Never had any trouble with him, and the orchard's not far away."

Elizabeth studied her daughter practically bobbing up and down in place, the extension cord from the phone stretched tight. "If you think it's all right...?"

Nathan met her gaze with warm assurance. "I think it will be fine."

"Well, okay, then," she told Claire, who did a little dance and a silent squeal. "You can go. But be home by ten."

Belle leaned toward the muscular, good-looking man with close-cropped hair beside her to speak above the commotion. "You've done a really great job in turning this place around these past few years."

Dan angled his handsome face to hers as kids milled by munching apple cider donuts and parents nursed cups of coffee. "I've had fun with it. Sure beats the heck out of dodging landmines in the desert."

Dan had come here after doing a second tour in Iraq. He'd left the Marines with distinction, having received the Purple Heart. Now he focused on achieving other accolades, like being named best apple producer in the valley. Perry coming to live with him last year had been a plus. After Perry's family tragedy, the boy had nowhere else to go and Dan had welcomed him with open arms. He genuinely seemed to care for his nephew and did as good a job of parenting as any biological father. Belle respected him for it, knowing firsthand the sorts of challenges he faced.

"How are things going with Melody?" he asked her. "I heard about that latest thing."

Belle frowned, figuring Perry had filled him in. "I sure wish she'd get over it—her penchant for stirring up trouble, that is."

"She'll outgrow it, sooner or later."

"Sooner would be best."

Dan laughed good-naturedly and eyed her with admiration. "You're a good mom. She'll come out okay, you'll see." He plucked two apples from a barrel beside him and handed one over. "The apple doesn't fall far from the tree."

She accepted one and took a bite. "We'll see." She spied Melody in the distance, laughing and cavorting with Joy and some other girls. They were piling onto a flatbed trailer hitched to a tractor, about to take a hayride. From this perspective, Melody appeared as normal and happy as any other girl. But Belle knew she was hurting on the inside. They'd tried a stint of family counseling, but that had only made Melody more stubbornly morose. She'd slammed herself in her room after every session, proclaiming to hate her mom for dragging her through it. Eventually, Nathan had convinced Belle that perhaps now wasn't the time to force Melody into therapy. So Belle had continued going herself, to gather tips on how to handle her daughter. How she wished Melody would pull out of it and begin to see some of the good in life. The only thing that appeared to bring her joy these days was causing others misery, and Belle's heart hung heavy with that knowledge.

"I don't want you to lose faith, Belle. It's always darkest before the dawn."

"Hope so."

Dan took her hand on the hay bale between them as they sat in companionable silence.

It felt good being here beside him, and his presence was a warm comfort. While they weren't technically dating, she and Dan had formed a sort of closeness that was more than friendship, but not quite intimate.

She'd gotten to know him slowly during the past several months, mostly through his regular trips to the library. She'd initially been impressed by how much he read, tearing through a whole stack of books every few days. She'd begun to think he'd surpass Martha in his rabid hunger for literature, until she pondered his reading list. The fact that he'd started with action adventure was no big surprise. By the time, he'd resorted to checking out nonfiction books on home decorating, though, she'd suspected his routine visits had less to do with books than they did with her. Each time he'd come by, he made sure to ask her opinion on something or another, or request her help researching gardening strategies for the orchard. Once she learned he'd grown up on one, Belle realized his pleas for help were all bunk. He equally didn't appear to be reading the books he'd been borrowing. At least not most of them in detail. She'd found several returned with one of Martha's old bookmarks in place, meaning that Martha had forgotten to remove them while Dan had never happened upon them at all. After a while, he'd asked her out for coffee. They'd even been to lunch a time or two. But mostly they talked over the counter at the library, in hushed tones so as not to disturb the others.

"You know what we should do sometime?" he asked her.

"What's that?"

"Go out to dinner."

Belle's heart leapt in her chest.

"A real dinner, I mean. You know, the sort where a waiter brings us wine?"

Heat warmed Belle's cheeks. She'd dreamed forever of him asking her but had never imagined he actually would.

"That would be fine. Some time."

He gently squeezed her hand and smiled. "It would, wouldn't it?"

Elizabeth watched Claire dash to the red pickup in the drive, hair flying behind her as she went. A cute, dark-haired boy waited in the cab. "Don't worry, Mrs. Jennings!" he called through his driver's side window. "I'll get her back safe and sound!"

A slight queasiness took hold as Elizabeth watched Claire slide in the truck, buckle up, and drive away, a happy grin on her face all the while. "Hoo boy." Her heart pinged and her throat muscles tightened.

"You doing okay?" Nathan asked from beside her. They stood on the porch as the old red truck chortled down the road, kicking up dust and tiny pebbles.

"I'll live," she replied, not entirely certain that was true. *My baby girl. Just like that! And it was only yesterday, it seemed, she first noticed boys…*

Nathan laid a steadying hand on her shoulder. "It was bound to happen someday."

"I know. I just wasn't prepared for some day to come so soon. You'd think I'd have some sort of warning."

"Teenagers don't talk much."

"Claire has always talked to me!"

"Hmm."

"What's that supposed to mean?"

"Just don't let it hurt your feelings if she suddenly stops."

"Suddenly, I'm not feeling so well."

"Why don't you have a seat here?" he said, motioning to one of the cushioned rattan chairs on the porch. "I'll bring you a glass of water."

"That would be great, thanks."

Elizabeth sank down in a chair, wondering where the years had gone. It seemed like only yesterday she was holding Claire's hand and walking her into her first day of kindergarten. Nathan returned with the water and shared a sympathetic smile.

"I don't want to impose on your time, but with Claire being out for the evening now, I'd hate to leave you alone."

Elizabeth blinked as she registered what he was saying. "Oh no, don't go! What I mean is, please stay. I'd rather not handle this evening alone."

"Should I bring us more coffee?"

"That would be super. Thanks, Nathan. There should be plenty in the pot."

Nathan strolled to the kitchen, considering this stroke of luck. While he'd badly wanted to spend time with Elizabeth and Claire, he hadn't hoped for time alone with Elizabeth. That was something he'd considered striving for later. Maybe after she got to know him a little more and trusted him a bit. He'd thought he might ask her out to lunch downtown one day while she was working and needing a break. There was so much about her he didn't know and wanted to learn, and had reasoned he'd get there, given some time. He just thanked his lucky stars he'd have the opportunity to start early. Nathan poured them two steaming mugs and carried them onto the porch.

She gave him a grateful smile. "I appreciate your staying awhile. It really helps with the transition. Having someone to talk to."

"There are a lot of nice folks in town. You'll be talking to them all before long."

"That may be the case," she said. "But in the meantime, I like who I'm talking to now."

Nathan felt the back of his neck warm but wasn't at all sure whether she was flirting. There was a nice crispness in the air as night settled in, a quarter moon angling over the graveyard. "Looks like we'll have a full moon for Halloween this year."

Elizabeth laughed. "What does that mean? That I have to worry about werewolves now?"

"Hardly." Nathan sipped from his mug. "Just that things should be nice and clear. Good for trick-or-treaters."

"I miss those days when Claire was small."

"You'll miss these days too."

"I know."

"I guess we've all got to savor what we've got while we can."

"Yes."

Elizabeth stared off in the distance, her gaze skimming the dark ridge of the mountains. "It really is a beautiful view, if you can forget that there are tombstones in the way."

"You travel much, Elizabeth?"

"Beg pardon?"

"Around the country. Or maybe abroad?"

She sighed and shook her head. "Never even been so far as over those mountains."

"Is that a fact?"

"Yeah. How about you?"

"A few years back I did some hiking. Camped my way across the entire US of A, all the way up into Yellowstone."

"Wow. That's impressive."

"I had a good time with it. It's what I wanted to do."

"Have any exciting experiences?"

"A few harrowing ones, yeah."

"Like?"

"Like the time I got stuck in Yosemite in a blizzard. Took the rangers a full ten days to dig me out."

"How did you survive it?"

"Wasn't easy, I can tell you that."

"What brought you to Blayton?"

"I'd known Bernie back in the day, and he spoke well of it. By then, Belle and Melody had moved here too. I guess I was looking for something to do, seeking to find my place. I'd trained at the police academy back home and served about ten years out of high school before deciding I'd had enough. It was rough work in the city, and I needed a break. A long break…away from sirens and neon lights, if you know what I'm saying."

"So you went on your big adventure. *Head west, young man.*"

"Exactly."

"Well, this certainly seems a good fit for you. You make an excellent town sheriff."

"Thanks for saying so."

He studied her a beat as night winds blew and the rockers creaked next door. "Do you think you'll ever do it?"

"What?"

"Go over those mountains," he said, motioning with his chin.

"I'd like to. Someday."

Nathan gazed in her eyes, and her heart gave a flutter. "Maybe someday I'll take you."

Claire drew a breath, absorbing the wonderful scents in the air…from fried apple donuts and funnel cake to hot apple cider and caramel apples. It was almost like a carnival but homespun and better, with a mime tying balloons into animal forms for children gathered by the side of a barn.

"This is really cool," she said to Perry as he led her through the rows of apple trees abutting the open field strung with festive lights. "Who knew Blayton had so much action?"

Perry smiled smugly and took her hand. "Come on. There's something I want you to see."

"Where are we going?" she asked. But her heart was totally light. So light, in fact, she felt it was filled with helium and she might float off into the night.

He led her into a shadowy grove that opened onto an enormous sky. "Here," he said, releasing his grip. "Away from the lights."

Claire stared up in awe at the glittery sky that seemed to be set with a million diamonds. "Awesome."

"Yeah. It's even better under a full moon. It's like the whole world lights up just for you."

She gave a saucy tilt to her chin. "One's coming, I hear."

"They pretty much do. Once a month."

"You must love living out here."

"It's cool, most of the time. But it's sort of far from everything."

"*Blayton's* far from everything."

"Yeah."

"I feel like I've stepped back in time."

"It's a little hard at first, but you'll get used to it."

She surveyed the lines of his face in the shadows. "I think I will."

"Ever been on a hay ride?" he asked her.

"Not in Richmond."

"Then maybe it's time."

Before long, Perry was helping Claire onto the trailer as other kids climbed down.

"Well, look who the cat dragged in," Melody said with a sneer, pushing past her.

Joy was close at her heels. "Wouldn't that be *out*?"

"Yeah, and it was Mrs. Fenton's cat, wasn't it?"

The other pair with them snickered.

"Hey, girls." Perry's voice was a friendly warning, a reminder to them that he was there.

Melody's face beamed brightly, then took on a cloudy cast as her gaze flitted to Claire. "Don't tell me that—?"

"Everyone's just here to have a good time," Perry told her. "Let's keep it that way, all right?"

She huffed and rolled her eyes at her companions, who shrugged in return. "Suit yourself. Though I've got to say," she spewed under her breath, "your taste's not all that."

Perry caught her by the elbow before she could step away. "I know you meant to pay me a compliment." Then he addressed the others. "Melody's just never been very good with words."

Her face flushed red as she turned abruptly away. "Let's go, guys," she said to her friends, who filed in suit and stormed after her. "She's cast a spell on him."

Joy's reply was a chortle. "Now she's got magical powers?"

Melody fumed and plowed ahead, not caring to lower her voice. "That's what happens when you live next to ghosts!"

"Whoa," Claire said, taking her seat. "Anger-management time."

Perry wedged himself between her and another kid who was sitting too close. "I'll say."

"What's her problem, anyway?"

"Sometimes she tries to cut it back. But Melody's meanness is like her fingernails. It always grows out again."

"Her friends seem to like her."

"Those girls are afraid of her. Afraid that if they don't do what she says, she'll turn against them and make their lives miserable too."

"That's a hard way to live," Claire said sadly.

"Yeah," Perry agreed as the wagon began to roll. "But let's not think about Melody anymore tonight."

"That's a deal!"

"Claire?"

"Huh?"

"Thanks for coming out with me. I mean, I know I called really late."

"I'm glad you called," she said. "Real glad."

His eyes warmed with surprise. "Yeah?"

"Yeah."

"Wow. That's nice."

Melody stood in the donut line with the other girls, watching the wagon roll away.

"Uh-oh," Joy quipped beside her. "I've seen that expression before."

"What are you going to do?" a third girl asked, her tone a tad gleeful.

Melody narrowed her gaze, still tracking the happy couple. "Teach that little witch a lesson."

A few minutes before ten, Claire breezed in the door, a blissful sparkle in her eye.

"So?" Elizabeth prodded. "How did everything go?"

"Okay."

"Just okay?"

Claire cupped her mouth with a giggle. "Oh, Mom, he's so cool."

"Perry?"

"Totally cool. You should have seen how he put those girls in their place."

Elizabeth's brow wrinkled with worry. "Is that Melody person still giving you trouble?"

"I can handle it."

"Seriously, honey. If it keeps up, maybe I can talk to Nathan. She's his niece, you—"

"*Mo-om! Puleeze.* I'd die."

"Well, we couldn't have that."

"No."

"Want something to eat?"

"I'm stuffed from apple donuts."

"Sounds yum."

"They were." Claire suddenly frowned. "I'm sorry. I should have brought you one. I didn't think to—"

"It's all right. I had plenty of apple cake to fill me up."

Claire glanced back toward the kitchen. "Nathan's gone, right? I didn't see his cruiser."

"Left about thirty minutes ago."

"That was a long cup of coffee."

"It was…nice."

"Um-hum."

"We just visited, that's all."

"I'm glad you're making friends."

"What do you mean?"

"Male friends. Ones of the opposite sex."

"I've had male friends!"

"Your boss, Jerry, doesn't count."

"Why not?"

"He's married."

"What's that go to do…" Her words fell off as Claire cocked an eyebrow.

"This is good for you."

"Why, thanks. I'm glad you approve."

"You're not getting any younger, you know."

"Claire!"

She broke out in giggles again. "I'm just yanking your chain."

"Yeah, and I feel it," Elizabeth said, but she could sense herself grinning just the same.

"So, you seeing Nathan again?"

"Everybody sees everybody in this town."

"You know what I mean."

Elizabeth flipped back her hair and tried to sound casual about it. "He might have said something about stopping by my shop next week to see how things are going."

Claire gripped her by the elbows. "Mom, that's great!"

"And…" Elizabeth added slyly. "He might have dropped a hint about taking me to lunch."

"Wow, Mom. Lunch. Better slow down there."

Elizabeth stared at her daughter, who sagely shook her head.

"Wouldn't want to move too fast."

Chapter Five

By Sunday, Elizabeth and Claire had done the last of their unpacking. They'd been too busy with work and school to deal with boxes during the week, so the few things they hadn't gotten to the weekend before they'd tackled today and yesterday. It was a gorgeous autumn afternoon, sunlight bouncing off the trees hedging the graveyard. Somehow even the cemetery appeared lovely set against the spectacular mountains, now in full bloom with October colors. The air was light and crisp as wind rippled through the trees, sending gold and brown leaves spiraling to the ground. Claire plucked at her guitar on the front porch while Elizabeth sipped hot coffee. Life was beginning to seem idyllic in this small town. It was uncanny how the two of them had settled in, and how much at home they were already starting to feel in just a short while.

"That's a nice tune you're playing."

Claire looked up from strumming. "Who knew I'd be playing to such an audience one day?" She glanced across the street at the tombstones. "At least no one's complaining."

Elizabeth smiled at her daughter, glad she'd developed a sense of humor over their living circumstances. They couldn't really be helped at this point and wouldn't have to last forever. Phantom raised his head from the porch railing with a lazy yawn. He'd found a spot in the sun and was enjoying keeping them company outdoors.

"Think we'll get a lot of snow here?" Claire asked.

"I'd guess a bit more than in Richmond."

"That's nice." She strummed her last few chords, then set down her guitar. "I won't mind it, you know. Getting snowed in here in Blayton, beside a haunted house."

Elizabeth laughed out loud. "If we get much of a winter, the ghosts themselves will be too cold to come out."

Claire's gaze panned the old Victorian next door. "Why do you think it hasn't sold?"

"It's an older place." Elizabeth shrugged. "Could need a bit of repair."

"At least the neighbors are good."

"World's best," Elizabeth agreed, raising her mug.

Phantom plopped down off the porch railing and climbed up onto Claire's lap, starting to purr.

"Looks like somebody agrees."

Claire stroked the cat's head, before addressing her mom. "When's the satellite dish going in?"

"Lex is coming by my office tomorrow and says he thinks he can get out here by the end of the week." Lexington Holt was Martha's husband. He also ran the only communications firm in Blayton. Satellite TV, Wi-Fi, or broadband. Whatever your interest, Lex was the man to fix you up.

"We'll get Internet then?"

Elizabeth crossed her fingers and held up her hand. "That's the plan."

"Great! I'd begun to think we'd fallen off the earth into some sort of black hole."

"Come on, Blayton's not that bad."

"You're right," she said, snuggling the cat. "It's not so terrible. Not so terrible, after all."

Curly-headed Janet adjusted her cat-eye glasses on the bridge of her nose and stared at the girls. She stood at the register while Melody and her friends dumped bags of fake spider webs and other items on the counter. "Ya'all are picking up quite a bit of Halloween stuff."

"We're, uh…helping to decorate for the Halloween dance," Joy offered. "The one at the high school."

Janet lifted the dismembered body part oozing with painted blood. "Nice. You got the severed foot. Is that the prize for best dancer?"

Melody stared at her dumbstruck. "Huh?"

"When someone can't dance, you say he has two left… Never mind."

Joy studied the rubber foot. "How can you tell which foot it is?"

"Forget about it," Janet said, ringing them up. "That will be thirty-six dollars even."

Probably the only thing Melody appreciated about Blayton was the fact that there was no sales tax here. Made it easy to shop within a budget. Especially at the Dollar Store. She and her three buds had each chipped in ten dollars toward their goal. It was a twofold project and would be every bit worth the investment. Melody felt devilish just thinking of how well it would go. Once their plan was executed, Perry would see Claire for the hysterical wimp she was. And Claire… Poor little thing… Would be bent on getting out of Dodge. So determined, in fact, she'd work to convince her mother, who by then would have also begun to suspect something wasn't quite right with this town.

"Mel!" Joy nudged her. "We're waiting for you to throw in your ten."

"Oh right. Sorry." She flashed a bright grin at Janet.

Janet bagged their stash with a dubious frown, then watched as they bunched in a giggling passel and headed out the door. "Have a nice day, girls."

Bernie leaned into the doorjamb of Nathan's office. It was Monday morning at nine o'clock. "There's something Janet told me this weekend that I think you ought to know."

Nathan, who'd been busy reviewing third-quarter revenues and expenses, looked up. "What's that?"

"Melody Anne and some of her friends were in the Dollar Store on Sunday buying supplies."

"What kind of supplies?" Martha asked, stepping up behind him. She knew the kids well enough to surmise that if Nathan's niece was up to something, Joy was right in the thick of it with her. They'd been best friends since the eighth grade.

"Halloween stuff," Bernie said. "Claimed they were decorating for the high school dance."

"That could be," Nathan told him. "There is a dance next Saturday."

Martha scrunched her lips, reflecting. "I thought the PTO took care of that."

Nathan addressed them both. "I'm not exactly seeing how a group of kids buying Halloween stuff in October is a crime."

"Janet says she got a funny feeling."

Nathan knew better than to respond to this. Janet was always getting funny feelings, having premonitions, and seeing people's auras in some weird shade. Nathan's color was ecru, which sounded more like a vegetable than a descriptive term to him. Not that he bothered to argue with Janet's assessments. She was always quite sure of herself when she made them. And Bernie, bless his faithful-husband soul, always backed her up. One hundred percent. In public, that was. Only Nathan knew privately that Bernie thought Janet's ideas were a little loopy sometimes. But she was a wonderful wife and one hell of a cook besides. So who was Bernie to quibble over a few minor quirks?

Nathan guessed Bernie didn't find kids buying Halloween stuff in October particularly unusual himself. But he also knew if something did go wrong and—heaven forbid—those kids pulled off some prank—Bernie would never hear the end of it for failing to heed Janet's hunch and pass on her suspicions. Nathan would never hear the end of things either, if word of this got back to Belle and he hadn't chosen to inform her about what, or what might not, be going on. *Ah, the joys of living in a small town.*

Nathan nodded. "Thanks, Bernie. I'll look into it." Then he lowered his head and got back to work, thinking this was going to be a long month.

Lex stood in Elizabeth's newspaper office, shaking his head at the blinking light on the router. "I'm not sure why that's not booting up. Could be the general server's still down."

"For everyone?" Elizabeth asked with dismay. "But how can that be?"

Lex was a tall, slim guy with a thinning hairline, yet his smile was warm as crinkles formed at the corners of his eyes. "I'm sorry, Mrs. Jennings. We had a big storm blow through here about a week ago. Must have been right before you moved over. High winds, hail. Tore everything up. Most of the poles leading out of town got hit. I know the fellows have been working on it. But a lot our communications systems are still mangled."

"How much longer could it take?"

"Hard to say. Could be a couple of hours. On the outside, a week. Maybe two."

Two weeks? "You don't understand. I'm under a deadline to get out my first edition."

He scratched his head a moment, then met her gaze. "Well, if it's the first one, then how will folks know it's late?"

"Jerry will know."

"Jerry?"

Elizabeth sighed heavily. "He's my boss in Richmond. I'll have to give him a call."

"Yes, ma'am."

"At least this won't affect setting up the broadband at home."

"Can't promise you that. The problems seem to be widespread. And the crew we've got working on it? They're a skeleton crew, if you know what I mean. Only three boys."

"That's all that's been assigned?"

"That's all that we've got."

"Has this happened before?"

"I kind of hate to say this, with this being my line of work and all, but telecommunications aren't exactly our strength in Blayton. When things are humming, they're good. But, every once in a while, we get surprised by Mother Nature. Not much to do about it other than allow the boys to do their job and sit tight."

Elizabeth's morning was going from bad to worse. All she needed was to have to face Claire after school with the news there'd be no social media for another few weeks. Claire was already feeling cut off from the world and missing her old friends. Kids that age didn't use traditional phone calling to stay in touch. Messages needed to be typed in at one-hundred-forty characters or less. "And the satellite TV?" she asked weakly.

"If you're getting the bundle, might behoove you to wait for me to make the service call. Otherwise, you'll be paying double what you should. Double the service and installation fees."

And paying double *for anything* wasn't something Elizabeth could consider doing at this moment. She'd come here with a set amount of money but wouldn't be paid again from headquarters until the end of this month. And that deposit was contingent on her first issue getting out. Elizabeth tried to think out how to make her grocery money stretch into the next month, but that seemed impossible. She'd need to call Jerry right away and ask for an extension. Surely, he'd be reasonable and understand. Jerry was a little crabby at times, but generally treated folks fairly. "You're right," she said to Lex. "I'll wait."

"Tell you what," he said kindly. "I'll do my best to tackle things quickly. Hopefully, I'll have you up and running here by this time tomorrow. And if it seems that service isn't affected in your residential area, I'll give you a call and get right on that too."

"That would be great," she said, writing down a number. "Better use my landline."

After Lex left, Elizabeth sat at her desk to call Jerry. She couldn't believe they had this old-school kind of telephone in here, the type with the round dial that clickety-clacked and spun around as you dialed each number. She'd tried to pick up a newer model in town, but no local stores carried that sort of thing. She would have had to drive seventy-five miles to the next larger town. And at this point, that hardly seemed worth it. She and Claire were already making up a list of all the modern-day provisions they would need. Things you couldn't get in Blayton. They planned to make a road trip of it too. They just hadn't set a precise date about when that might be.

Finally, Elizabeth seemed to be connecting. The ringing began as a distant tone beyond a crackling connection. She waited as the phone rang three, then four times. After the fifth ring, she was about to give up. Then Jerry answered at last.

"Jerry Walker," he said in his matter-of-fact tone.

"Jerry! Thank God. I was beginning to think you wouldn't—"

"Hello? Hello? Is somebody there?"

Elizabeth cradled the handset, drawing the mouthpiece toward her lips. "Jerry? Can you hear me?"

"I'm sorry," he said, dismissing her. "Must be a bad connection."

"Wait!"

But it was too late. Elizabeth already heard a dial tone.

She punched the disconnect button, then tried again, receiving no better results. *Wonderful,* she thought, staring at the antiquated piece of equipment. *What do I do now?*

"Can I help you with something?" Nathan asked, walking in. He'd apparently read her troubled expression.

Elizabeth was glad to see a friendly face. She was having a rotten day. "Communications issues," she said, setting the handset back in its cradle.

"Phone's not working?"

"Not getting through. To Richmond, I mean. I was trying to call my boss there, Jerry."

"Maybe I can ask Lex to have a look at your connection."

"Lex has already been by."

"That's great! You've got your Internet, then?"

Elizabeth frowned. "Not for another week or two. At best."

"Ouch." Nathan grimaced in understanding. "Aren't you supposed to get that first edition out?"

"Guess it will have to be late."

"Better late than never." He shot her an encouraging smile. "Hey, I'll tell you what. Let me get you out of here for a little while to brighten your mood."

"What did you have in mind?"

"Everything seems better after a hot Italian sub and french fries."

Elizabeth's stomach did a little rumble, and she realized for the first time that she'd skipped breakfast. She'd packed a bagel to eat at the office but had become so caught up in trying to work out communications issues with Lex, she'd completely forgotten about it. "Who serves that?"

"Small deli around the corner."

"Sounds terrific."

Claire walked to her locker to stow the books from her morning classes and retrieve the next set. It seemed an unnecessary inconvenience having to do this. Back in Richmond, kids didn't even use their lockers. Everyone toted everything in the backpacks they kept perpetually slung over their shoulders. But Blayton High had a strictly enforced *No Backpacks in the Classroom* rule. This supposedly cut down on kids sneaking in cell phones. But seriously? With the awful cell service in this town, who was there to call? Claire laid her hand on the metal latch that opened her locker, but it appeared stuck. She tried it again—pushing harder. *That's weird. What's going on?*

Claire placed her books on the floor, then gave the handle a shove with both hands. *Click.* It popped open. But something pressed against the locker door from the inside. Something weighty bursting to get—

"*Owww!*" Claire shouted, bolting backward as a witch's loud voice erupted in cackling laughter and a hellacious amount of stuff spilled forward: vampire teeth, fake spiders, ogling gooey eyeballs, and *what's that?* An amputated foot all sprang from her locker and careened toward the floor. A crowd of teens quickly gathered to gawk at the mess on the floor and the interior of Claire's howling locker that was draped in sticky cobwebs. Claire felt her face flash hot as others hooted and stared, and a host of Halloween sounds continued, ranging from a woman's tortured cries to ghouls clanking chains. She set her jaw and drew a breath, willing herself not to acknowledge any of them. Instead, she calmly reached in the locker and pulled the tiny noise box from the joint below the locker's hinge. Locating the switch, she turned it off, silencing the ghostly sounds.

At the far end of the hall, Melody and her friends backed around the corner in giggles.

"That was amazing," Penelope proclaimed.

"Yeah," Lilly agreed. "Awesome."

Joy peered through the crowd at Claire, who seemed to reach up and wipe her cheek as she scooped her books off the floor. "Are you sure it wasn't too much?"

"What are you doing, Joy?" Melody asked. "Wimping out on us?"

"No, it's just that I didn't expect so many others to show up."

"All the better," Melody quipped. "And to think, this was only Phase I." She turned to the others with a grin. "Ready to get your spook on?"

Nathan set down his sub as Elizabeth bit into hers. Man, it was delicious. All hot and cheesy with heaps of meat, pickles, mustard, and mayo. Just the way she liked it.

"And so, I was thinking," he said, dabbing his mouth with a napkin, "with the leaves turning and all, now might be a good time to take you up on the trail."

"You mean into the Blue Ridge?"

"Shenandoah Parkway," he explained. "Not much of a drive from here. Twenty minutes, tops. We can make it up and back in one afternoon." He studied her with a smile, hazel eyes twinkling. "I could pack us a lunch. We'll be back well before Claire gets home from school."

Elizabeth sipped from her tea. "You mean, you want to go this week?"

"No time like Thursday."

"Why Thursday?"

"Bernie's taking over. It's my full day off."

"Not even on call?"

"Not even."

"I don't know. I've got to—"

"Sit around waiting for Lex to drop by? You can leave a key with Martha. She'll let him in if you'd like."

Elizabeth met Nathan's eyes, which still were on hers. "You're making it awfully hard to say no."

"Precisely my intention."

Elizabeth cocked her chin to the side, considering his offer. While she'd liked Nathan from the start, each time she was around him, she liked him even better. Plus, she was beginning to think that Claire was right. He must kind of like her to ask her on a hiking expedition. That went beyond friendly, in her book. Having lunch together in town was one thing. Being all alone out in nature…just the two of them…could spell something different. Something more like male-female interest. Elizabeth drew a deep breath, hoping she was ready for this. Then again, she knew she'd never forgive herself if she said no. Heck, Claire might not forgive her either. Her daughter's words came back to her. *"You're not getting any younger, you know."*

"How shall I dress for this day in the woods?"

His lips broke into a grin. "Sturdy shoes and jeans will do. You might want to pack a jacket in case it gets cool. I'll bring the rest of it."

When Claire burst through the front door later that afternoon, Elizabeth could have sworn it wasn't her child but a wild tornado. "Claire?" she inquired as Claire dropped her backpack to the floor and stormed up the stairs. "Honey, what's wrong?"

"I don't want to talk about it!" the girl shouted, shutting her door. But her tone said something had gone very wrong indeed.

Elizabeth was just about to head upstairs after her when the doorbell rang. She peeked outside and saw it was Perry.

"Perry, what's wrong? Did you and Claire have a fight?"

He thumbed his chest. "Me and...? No ma'am, not at all."

"Then why...?" Her gaze traveled upstairs, where she could faintly hear Claire sobbing.

"Do you think it'd be all right if I talked to her?"

"I don't know. She doesn't seem to feel much like talking."

Perry studied her with sincere brown eyes. "I think I might know a way to help."

It took some coaxing, but after a short interval during which she washed her face and received a motherly hug, Claire finally came downstairs. Elizabeth left her to speak privately with Perry in the living room, and went to work on dinner.

Just when she thought things were going so well, something terrible seemed to have happened. Elizabeth was grateful at least that Perry hadn't been part of it. Nathan had been right in his assurances about him. Perry was a good kid, and Elizabeth was glad he'd befriended her daughter. Sometimes all it took was one good friend to get you through the dark times. Elizabeth knew this from her own experience as a high school teenager. Like Claire, she'd been the new kid in town. Only her family had moved to Virginia from the North, making Elizabeth notable for her Delaware accent. She hadn't even realized she had one until a mean clique of girls started teasing her about it. Betsy Jean had stepped in with her sassy Southern loudmouth, telling them all where they could go and what they could do with it. The fact that she'd said it in her deep Georgia drawl had lent it that much more punch.

Elizabeth married right out of high school, and Betsy Jean went away to college. They lost touch over the years, but in those early days, they'd stuck tightly together. Eventually, they'd become a popular duo in their own right, both working as co-editors of their high school yearbook and picking up several admirers. Although they'd each been picked on as newcomers in the school, both had made a pact to be nothing but kind to others, including to the kids who'd initially tormented them. This somehow turned everything around. And by the time Elizabeth and Betsy Jean graduated at the top of their class, no one could barely even remember the names of those other girls or whether they'd contributed anything significant to the school at all.

Elizabeth stared out her kitchen window at the empty house next door with a deep sense of sadness. She wondered what Betsy Jean was up to now, or if she'd ever

have occasion to see her again. When Elizabeth married
Cash, Betsy Jean had been her maid of honor. It was sad
how lives and circumstances could drive close friends
apart. But during the bitterness of Elizabeth's divorce,
she'd unintentionally become severed from everybody.
Even though she'd moved two states away by then, Betsy
Jean had tried to call—and to help. But Elizabeth had felt
so closed in, the last thing she had the strength to do was
reach out to a lifeline from far away.

Cash's weekend binge drinking quickly morphed into
full-scale alcoholism. Fearing for her baby's safety,
Elizabeth fled to a hotel with Claire more than once to
avoid a drunken rage. The time Cash pulled out his baseball
bat and started dismantling the nursery had been the final
straw. This time when she left the house with Claire,
Elizabeth had no intention of coming back. She'd tried to
get Cash help and had attended meetings herself. But Cash
wasn't interested in giving any more than lip service to
getting better. Largely because he didn't believe he had a
problem. Everybody had too much now and again. And so,
yeah. Maybe he had a tiny temper. A temper that had cost
him his job, and eventually his family. After the divorce
went through, Cash left town and never returned. They'd
all turned their backs on him, he'd said. Every last one of
them. Nobody knew where he'd gone; not even his brother
or aging parents had a clue. All they said they could do was
pray for him to eventually turn his life around, though
Elizabeth had given up on that prayer years before.

She felt something damp on her cheeks and realized
she'd been crying. Weeping over so much time lost and the
grief it had caused her baby girl. Elizabeth picked up a
dishtowel to wipe her tears, knowing she'd done the right
thing. The brave thing. And the best thing for her and little
Claire. It hadn't been easy getting by as a single mother.

She'd worked days at a diner to put herself through night school so she could earn a journalism degree. But at least she could ensure a household that was safe and sane for the two of them. For the first few years after the divorce, she'd lived in fear that Cash might come storming back. Break into the house some evening in a drunken fit and threaten them both. But that worry eased with each passing season. And now it was fall. Elizabeth watched as the last of the golden-brown leaves spiraled to the ground from the towering oak next door. Autumn, the season that signaled the ending of summer and the ushering in of colder days. But somehow here, in Blayton, Elizabeth knew that she and Claire would stay safe and warm. For there was nothing better than being where you were meant to be. In some strange way, Elizabeth felt as if someone had preordained it. Although she hadn't known it existed until a few short weeks before, Blayton, Virginia already seemed like home. For home was where the heart was, and, after so many years in tumult, Elizabeth's heart was finally starting to feel at peace.

Perry sat next to Claire on the sofa. "I mean it," he told her firmly. "I think it will work."

Claire stared at him in disbelief. "So, what? I should just walk straight up and ask her?"

"Yeah."

"*Why are you being so mean to me?*"

"What's she going to say?"

"Some excuse."

"There *is* no excuse, and you know that. That's why I'm saying you should do it. Call her on it."

"I don't know, Perry. That sounds…"

"What?"

"Like a long shot."

"Okay, then take the other route."

"Reporting her to the principal? I don't think so. That will only backfire on me."

"It could."

"Besides. I really have no proof it was her."

"But you *know* it was her. So do I."

"Yeah, but it's not like she left fingerprint evidence."

"Maybe she did."

Claire laughed. "Come on, Perry. This isn't some crime show. It's Blayton High!"

He hung his head. "You're right." But when he looked up, he was grinning. "You're going to do it, aren't you?"

Claire sat up a little straighter on the sofa, feeling her confidence surge. "I might."

"It will work. I'll guarantee it."

"And if it doesn't?"

"Well, then, what will you have lost?"

"A lot of face, probably. Like this one here," she said, patting her left cheek. "And my better side here," she said, patting her right.

Perry surprised her by leaning forward and giving her a quick peck on her cheek. Her skin flashed hot, tingling from the sweet pressure of his lips. Claire had never kissed a boy before and certainly had never had one kiss her. Even on the cheek!

"Perry! What was that for?"

"Well, if you're going to lose it…" he said, drawing out the words, "I thought I should probably get a little sample first."

Claire burst out laughing. "You're bad."

"Nope. I'm actually pretty good. One of the best guys at school."

Claire blushed. "All right. I'll give you that."

"I'm proud of you, Claire."

"Proud?"

"Look at you, walking into a new school. Putting up with those bullies. Not just putting up. Pushing back."

Claire crossed her arms in front of herself. "You really know how to put the pressure on."

"I only want to help."

"I know."

She surveyed him a lingering moment. "What makes you want to be so nice to me?"

"No special reason… Other than you're probably the most amazing girl I've ever met."

Claire's pulse raced and little butterflies flitted all about in her stomach. "Really?"

He leaned toward her with a soft whisper. "Really."

Claire pressed her palm to his chest and pushed him back. "You'd better leave before you kiss me again." Steam rose from her cheeks. "Or I kiss you… Or yeah… Something."

Perry cocked his chin with a smile as Elizabeth peered into the room. "Everything okay in here?"

"Um-hum, yeah," both of them said, scooting apart and sitting up straighter.

"Good," Elizabeth chirped, glancing from one to the other. "Just checking."

Chapter Six

A few days later, before the first bell, Claire steeled her nerves. *You can do this. Yeah, sure. If Perry thinks you can do it, you can.* Melody and her friends gathered outside the cafeteria, swapping jokes by the soda machine. Claire steadied the backpack on her shoulder and trudged ahead, mentally rehearsing what she would say. But the moment Melody turned her cold blue stare on her, the script flew out the window.

"Ah, can I talk to you a minute?"

The blonde angled toward her and puffed out a word. "Boo!"

The girls around her laughed.

"I meant, alone."

Melody raised her brow. "Well, well. Look who's not afraid."

"We'll see about that," Penelope sneered.

"Yeah," a shorter girl added.

Joy's lips twisted in a frown. "Why don't you hear her out?"

Melody glanced at Joy with exasperation.

"It will just take a minute," Claire said.

Melody shrugged at the others, then handed Joy her backpack to hold. "Shouldn't take more than a second. Can't imagine she's got much to say," she told the others, striding away. Once they stood off to the side, she snapped at Claire. "What exactly is your problem?"

Claire met her stare. "I'm not sure why, but it appears to be you."

"I don't have to listen to this." She tried to turn away, but Claire caught her arm. Melody narrowed her eyes in warning.

"I'm sorry," Claire said, releasing her. "I just really need for you... Want you to hear this."

"Hear what?"

Claire dropped her backpack to the floor and plowed ahead, willing her voice to remain steady. To her surprise, it came out nice and even, despite the tremors welling within her. "I'm not sure what I did. I mean, when I first got here. But, obviously, it was something to offend you. So..." She drew a breath and released it. "I want to apologize."

"*What?*" Melody lowered her voice in a whisper. "Are you out of your mind? You don't apologize to me. *I'm* the one who's been razzing you."

Claire felt a new surge of calm, as if the tables were turning somehow. "And, why *is* that?"

"I don't know what you mean."

"I mean, if I didn't do something to you... And I was almost sure that I had—"

"What could you have possibly done to me?" Melody hissed.

"Date Perry?"

"Hah! As if..." She rolled her eyes, then leaned closer. "That's not what Perry thinks, is it?"

"I don't know what he thinks. About you, I mean."

"Has he said something? About me?"

"Only that you're a lot nicer than you come across."

There was a rush of color at Melody's temples before her expression hardened again. "Yeah, well. If I were you, I wouldn't believe it."

Claire had her on the hook now and only had to reel her in. "So…if it's not my friendship with Perry that got you mad at me, what is it?"

Melody's face registered surprise. "Mad? Who said anything about me being mad at you?"

"I just figured… From how you've been acting."

"Look," Melody told her. "You're the new girl in town, all right. I get that." She glanced at her friends. "We all get that. But when you got here, it's important for you to know, you walked into a certain…order of things."

"Like a hierarchy?"

"Yeah. Whatever that means. So, as long as we're straight on that, you've got nothing to worry about. You don't have to go home crying to Daddy."

Claire pursed her lips hard to fight back the sting in her eyes. When she spoke, there was a hard edge to her voice. "There *is no* Daddy, for your information. And there hasn't been for a long time."

Melody held her tongue.

"Forget it," Claire said. "This was a really stupid idea."

She spun away from the crowd and headed in the opposite direction, thinking what an idiot she was. There she'd stood, sucking up to probably the most vicious girl in school, and all she'd gotten out of it were more barbs.

"Wait!" Melody cried, chasing after her.

Claire glanced back over her shoulder to see Melody running up with her backpack.

"You forgot this."

When she passed the backpack over, there was something different in her eyes. Something Claire hadn't seen there before. It was almost like Melody had the capacity to be a real person.

Nathan scraped another perfectly done hamburger off the grill and set on the plate Belle held beside him.

"This will be one of our last good evenings for cooking out," she told him.

"Nonsense," he said. "Grilling out's always a good idea. Don't even mind it in snow boots."

His sister laughed. "I forgot what a die-hard you are."

"You can call me Mountain Man Nathan, if you'd like."

"You haven't been up in the mountains in quite some time."

"True. Though that's about to change."

Belle's brow rose with interest. "Taking time off?"

"Just a day. But I'm due it, anyway."

"Darn," she said with disappointment. "I was hoping you were whisking that new girlfriend of yours away somewhere."

The tips of his ears felt as hot as those coals. "Girl…? Girlfriend?"

She waited until he set the last of the burgers on the platter then placed the lid on the grill. "Come now, brother. Fess up. Town talk is you were having lunch the other day. *And* I know firsthand she invited you to dinner."

"*And* I've got a very nosy sister," he teased. "Who, not so incidentally, has also been going out to dinner. At *Victor's Italian Restaurant*."

She swatted him with a potholder. "We're just friends. Good friends. You know that."

"Can you say candlelight? Violins? A romantic table for two? And there I was thinking old Dan had some kind of reading addiction." He winked at his sister. "Sounds more like an obsession for the librarian."

"Quit trying to change the subject."

He picked up his grilling supplies and carried them in the house as she followed after him. When they got to the kitchen, she set the platter on the counter with a suspicious look. "Who are you going hiking with?"

"Uncle Nathan!" Melody cried, running toward him with a hug. "I didn't know you were coming over tonight."

"Your mom invited me—to do the grilling. Wasn't that nice of her?"

"Superb."

Melody hugged him tighter as he cast a glance at Belle. Something was going on here, but he wasn't sure what. Belle sensed it too.

"Everything go okay in school today?"

"Oh yeah, just fine." She strode to the kitchen table and lifted a huge chocolate chip cookie. "Yum. Uncle Nathan bring these?"

"Not until *after* dinner," Belle said.

Melody returned the cookie to its plate with a frown. "How much longer?"

"Ten minutes. Time enough for you to set the table."

The teen sighed audibly, and Nathan chuckled. It was then that he remembered his mission. "Belle," he told her once his niece was out of earshot. "Janet saw something at the Dollar Store she wanted me to mention to you."

"Uh-oh." When her brother said *something*, it had apparently sounded more like *someone* to her.

"Could be nothing." He lowered his voice so Melody wouldn't hear. "Just Melody Anne and her friends buying lots of spooky stuff."

"For?"

"They claimed, the high school dance."

"That's odd. Melody hasn't mentioned a thing about it."

"If it were legit, wouldn't she have been hitting you up for the cash?"

Their gazes trailed toward the dining room.

"Just forks and knives tonight?" Melody asked.

"That's fine, hon!" Belle called. "And don't forget the condiments."

"I'll find a way to casually mention it at dinner," Nathan told Belle.

On the other side of town, Elizabeth and Claire carried their plates of pasta salad to the front porch. "Are you sure you don't mind being out here?" Elizabeth asked.

"No. It's a great night for eating outside."

"Pretty with the sun going down."

Claire set down her fork and studied the view. "You know, I don't even see them anymore."

"What?"

"The tombstones."

"Huh?"

"I mean, of course I know they're there. I just don't think of them the way I used to."

"As creepy?"

"I guess."

"Everyone needs a final place to be."

"I know. And those guys probably didn't pick it."

"What do you mean?"

"It was their families, don't you think?"

"Maybe."

Something creaked next door, and the women glanced across the way to see Phantom had jumped up onto an old rocker, sending it teetering back and forth. "Phantom!" Claire called. "Come away from there! Here, kitty, kitty!"

He sprang out of the chair, sending it rocking even harder. *Creak-crack, creak-crack, creak-crack* against the floorboards of the old front porch.

"And to think we used to be afraid of that too," Elizabeth said with a laugh.

"Speak for yourself."

"Hah!"

"Seriously, Mom. I had no worries about it."

"Hmm. If you say so, sweet daughter of mine."

Phantom sauntered over and curled around Claire's legs, whining softly for a piece of chicken.

"Claire Jennings," Elizabeth warned sternly. "Don't you dare feed that cat off of your plate."

"Aw, Mom," Claire said, "Wasn't about to do that." Then when her Mom turned her head, she passed Phantom a tiny morsel. He purred louder and sat down on his haunches, gazing up expectantly.

"Claire," Elizabeth said, "now you're teaching him to beg!"

But she couldn't help it. Phantom was so darn cute, and such a baby cat too. He crawled up in her bed each night, tucking himself in under her arm. Claire had never owned a pet before. Although it was something she'd always wanted. Something like a full-fledged family with a father, but she'd never in a million years tell her mom that. Claire knew her mom loved her deeply, and understood she'd moved heaven and earth to provide the best life for her she could. But sometimes there were gaps. Times when it would have been good to have a dad around to step in. The way Nathan had when her mom had hesitated about letting her go out with Perry that very first time. Nathan was a good guy. Pleasant enough to be around and stable in a laid-back way. She could tell that her mom liked him, and vice versa. That was for sure.

"You have any plans to see Nathan?"

"What made you think of him?"

Claire shrugged. "Just had a craving for chocolate chip cookies."

Elizabeth laughed. "We can't go taking advantage now. Nathan doesn't have to bake for us at every turn."

"No, he doesn't," Claire agreed. "But he can still come over."

Elizabeth studied her with surprise.

"Hang out. Whatever. It's all right, Mom. I understand."

"Well, thanks. Perry can come over too. Hang out, I mean."

"Might start getting crowded around here."

Elizabeth surveyed the mountains with a happy sigh. She'd thought of nothing but Nathan since their last lunch together and could scarcely wait until their date tomorrow. "It could at that."

"You look good, Mom," Claire said.

Elizabeth playfully flipped back her hair. "You mean, *hot*?"

"That too, but there's more to it. Something else now."

"Yeah? What?"

"You seem… I don't know, younger?"

Elizabeth preened, liking this sound of this.

"Yeah, hopeful somehow."

"Hopeful?"

"I don't know why, but that word fits."

Yes, Elizabeth found herself thinking, *it certainly does.* And Elizabeth Jennings hadn't felt hopeful in such a long while, she'd nearly forgotten what that feeling was.

Nathan reached over to grab the potato salad. "I hope you don't mind my asking," he said, addressing his niece, "but have you got a date to the dance?"

Melody Anne flushed. "I don't even have a boyfriend, Uncle Nathan."

"Oh, that's right. I'm sorry."

"Kids all go in groups these days," Belle told him. "I think I like it better that way."

"Hmm, yes. Can't say I disagree. This potato salad is delicious, by the way," he said, ladling up another scoop.

"Why, thanks," Belle returned before he continued.

"So how's it all coming together?" he asked the girl.

"How's what coming together?"

"The dance."

"I'm not sure how I'm supposed to…"

Belle widened her eyes at Nathan, and Melody Anne stopped talking.

"Is something going on here?" she asked after a pause.

"Not really," Nathan said, loading up a forkful. "It's just that Bernie heard you and some friends were helping decorate."

"You mean he heard that from Janet."

"Could be. Yes. Yes, I think that's right." He turned his gaze on hers. "So, are you? Helping decorate?"

"I… We haven't decided yet."

"But the dance is just three days away!" Belle broke in.

Melody Anne shifted in her chair. "We got the stuff thinking we were, but then another team stepped in."

Belle studied her daughter. "Team?"

Melody Anne rolled her eyes toward the kitchen, and Nathan could tell she was thinking fast. "There was a contest at school. Winning team gets to decorate. Losers help clean up. Something like that. Not sure of all the details. Anyway. Fact is, we *thought* we had won. Went out, bought all the stuff and everything. Turns out there was a miscount after all."

Nathan slowly raised an eyebrow. "So then, you're helping clean up?"

"Nope," the girl answered quickly. "Didn't win that one either."

Belle glanced at Nathan, then stared at her daughter. "Melody Anne, if I learn for one second that you were up to—"

But Nathan stopped her by calmly shaking his head. "No need to go jumping to any conclusions, here. We both know our Melody Anne is a sweetheart." He reached across the table and warmly patted her hand. "I want you to be especially nice to that new girl, Claire Jennings, you hear? She and her mom have been through some tough times. Having to leave their old home behind, settle into a new place…" He glanced around the table, then met her eyes. "I think we all know what that's like."

Melody swallowed hard and finished her meal in silence But Nathan knew she'd heard him all the same.

Chapter Seven

The next day, Melody met her group of friends in the cafeteria at their regular table.

"So, it's tonight, right?" Penelope asked her. They'd been planning it all week, and Thursday was their target date. If things went right and Claire freaked as much as they hoped she would, she'd want nothing more to do with Blayton High. Nothing to do with Blayton, period. Which would mean she'd tell Perry on Friday she was no longer going to the dance. That would give him time to ask out Melody. Or, at the very least, allow him to go stag so he could ask her to dance.

Joy glanced uncertainly around the table. "I was thinking maybe we should wait."

Melody didn't know what it was with Joy. It was like she no longer thought the things they did were ultra cool. But still, she went along for the ride. It was only recently that she'd begun to voice some dissent. This irked Melody no end, because she was already having doubts of her own. She didn't need things made overly complicated by having more misgivings heaped upon her. "What are you talking about, Joy?"

"Only that, if it's ghosts we're playing, shouldn't we wait until closer to Halloween?"

"It's only a week away."

"I meant, until Halloween."

"Don't be stupid," Penelope said. "Even *I'm* not going in a haunted house on Halloween to play the undead."

"Me either," another girl, Lilly, agreed.

The truth was, Melody didn't much want a part of that herself. Not that she really believed in ghosts or anything. It just seemed kind of like tempting fate to call them out on the actual day. Night. All Hallows Eve. Whatever. "The point is, we were to get this done *before* the dance."

"Oh, right."

"Yeah."

"I'm still not sure about it," Joy said. "It feels kind of sacrilegious to me."

Melody fumed at her friend. "If that's how you all feel, then let's not do it!" On the outside, she was blustery, but on the inside, Melody felt the slightest twinge of relief. If the others chickened out, she wouldn't have to go through with it. They could call the whole thing off, and make it seem like a mutual deal. Then she wouldn't get in trouble with her uncle, her mom, or anyone else. Plus, she wouldn't still be picking on Claire, which had started feeling less and less like a fun idea.

Penelope eyed the others combatively. "*I'm* not chickening out, if that's what you're saying."

Melody met Penelope's chilly green stare, seeing her own reflection in the other girl's eyes. Penelope appeared almost gleeful at the prospect of upsetting another kid. It was like it got her juices going just at the thought of it. Melody had never understood how unappealing that looked until she'd glimpsed it from the outside. Her stomach roiled at the notion that others in the school saw her like she saw Penelope now. "Nobody's chickening out. But maybe Joy is right. Maybe we should give this some time."

"But we already got all the stuff," Lilly said.

Penelope glanced at the others. "And I'm babysitting tomorrow."

Melody shivered at that thought, then turned her attention to the group. It was plain she wasn't getting out of this. She was in too deep already. While it was true she wasn't as pumped about it as she'd been at first, it honestly wasn't more than a harmless prank. One that might cause a few goose bumps and chills. And, oh yeah, make her archenemy Claire want to leave town. That.

Melody tried to forget the look in Claire's eyes as she'd pulled her aside to apologize. *"Have I done something to offend you?"* Only by showing up and being alive. Melody felt her heart harden again, the one that had temporarily—and inexplicably—gone soft.

"Okay," she said, lowering her voice to a whisper. "Tonight, at the Fenton place. Here's what we're going to do…"

Perry met Claire outdoors at their customary table. "Hey, Sunshine. What's cooking?" He studied her lunch. "Peanut butter and jelly again?"

"Ah, but it's peanut butter with *apple* butter this time. From your uncle's orchard."

Perry took his seat with a grin. "Awesome. Where'd you get that?"

"My mom picked it up at Evan's." Evan's was the town grocery store that carried local produce.

"That's cool," he said, unwrapping another fabulous lunch.

Claire took a bite of her sandwich, feeling slightly less envious. The apple butter wasn't just good. It *rocked.* "So, what time are you picking me up on Saturday?"

"Seven forty-five. Is that all right? The dance starts at seven thirty, but they say it's lame to show right on time."

"Sounds perfect."

She'd been thrilled he'd asked her to the dance, like on a real date and everything. Most of the girls going, who were going with guys at all, were meeting their dates at the door. Then again, most boys in their grade didn't drive. Claire was just lucky Perry was older. She was also grateful her mom had said yes. She had an inkling her mom had flown it by Nathan and he'd said something like, *Why not? It's only a dance. I'll bet you went to a dance or two at Claire's age.*

"So, guess where my mom is?"

"Now?"

"Yeah."

Claire leaned forward on her elbows. "On an outing."

"With Nathan?"

"Somewhere up there." Her gaze trailed to the mountains hedging the school's large ball fields.

"Sweet. Mrs. Jennings, the nature girl."

"Shut up!" She playfully slapped his arm. "Mom's never done anything like that before."

"Never?" Perry appeared amused. "Hope she told Nathan that."

Elizabeth gazed up at Nathan, who stood at the high end of the rope. He'd used it to shimmy up some kind of boulder that stood maybe fifteen feet tall. Then had secured the end of it around a tree, and now was encouraging her to do the same. "You're kidding me, right?"

"I thought you told me you'd been climbing before?"

"Hiking. You said hiking! You know, like the dwarves in the forest with their pick axes?"

"It's not such a big deal, really. You can do it, come on! And the view is astounding from here!"

He shot her an encouraging grin, and her heart fluttered. She wasn't sure if it was from his smile or from the altitude. Either way, she couldn't see herself shimmying up that boulder using nothing but this rope. The climb was practically vertical, for heaven's sake!

She gripped the rope, and her knees quaked. "Um, I'm not so sure…"

"Hang on!" he told her. "Stay right there! I'm coming down."

In an instant, he'd scaled down the rock like it was nothing, then grabbed her beneath her legs. "Nathan!" she cried with surprise. "What on earth are you doing?"

"Giving you a boost!" he said, heaving her skyward. "Hi-ho, hi-ho… Now grab the rope like a good Snow White."

"I don't think Snow White ever did this!"

"I don't think any of her dwarves had my stamina," he said, heaving a breath and hoisting her higher. "Now, Elizabeth! Go!"

In a flash of panic, she reached ahead of her and clung to her lifeline. "Keeping moving," he told her. "It's the best way to avoid the wasps!"

"Wasps?" she shrieked, wrapping hand over fist, her sneakers scuttling up rocky terrain as Nathan pressed her bottom skyward from below.

"Don't worry. I don't think they can hit a moving target!"

"What?"

"Heave ho!" He gave a final push then sent Elizabeth scuttling with all her might. Goodness knew, she hated stinging creatures. Especially when they stung in swarms.

Seconds later, she pulled herself up upon the flat-topped rock by the rope Nathan had secured around a sturdy tree. She was out of breath and in a sweat when Nathan joined her, not the least bit worn from the journey himself. "What about the bees?" she asked.

"Huh?"

"Wasps! Whatever."

"Oh, that! Just funning with ya on that small stuff."

"Nathan Thorpe, that wasn't very funny at all."

"Got you up here, didn't I?"

She huffed and set a hand on her hip. "Isn't it against some code of conduct for an officer of the law to fib?"

He shrugged and passed her some water. "I'm off duty."

She took a long, cool swig, her heartbeat finally calming down. She'd never thought she'd make it, but once she had, Elizabeth felt exhilarated. It was probably just the adrenaline. That stuff that cranked in when you feared you were on the verge of death.

"Come over here," Nathan encouraged. "I want you to see this."

She joined him near the precipice's edge without standing too close. "Wow! You can see the whole valley. It's gorgeous."

"Especially this time of year."

With the view bathed in fall colors, it was true. "Which way is Blayton?"

"Right down there," he said, motioning past a broad stand of trees.

"Where? I can't see it."

"It's so small it's hard to make out."

"What about the cemetery?"

"It's on the far side of that forest."

"Funny how everything looks different from here."

"In a good way, yeah?"

Elizabeth felt her head swoon and took a step backward away from the edge.

"Are you feeling okay?"

"Just a little lightheaded."

"Maybe you should sit down. Even at this level, the altitude change can get to you if you're not used to it."

Although her pulse had slowed, taking a breather seemed like a fine idea. Nathan offered her a hand and helped ease her down until she sat steadily on the rock's surface. "This is fantastic," she said, glancing around. "Really fantastic. I didn't even know I had it in me!"

Nathan smiled. "Rock climbing?"

"Doing something like this!" She motioned to the sweeping panorama. "You don't get this on pay-per-view."

"No, you don't."

After her nerves had calmed down and her head had cleared, she turned to him. "You know what I feel like?"

"No, what?"

"Like this was one of those *once in a lifetime experiences* I was meant to have."

"Is that so?" he asked, his face glowing in the sunshine. Warm breezes blew all around them, rippling through the brittle trees. "Then I'm awfully glad you're having it with me."

"Yeah," she said warmly. "Me too."

Nathan couldn't believe what a good sport Elizabeth was being. From their previous conversations, he hadn't figured her for a very adventuresome outdoorswoman, so he'd thought he'd tailored his activities accordingly. Who knew such a teeny scramble could incite so much panic? He was glad he'd gotten her through it so she could see the other side. Because the other side of fear was truly beautiful. It was a view that spoke of freedom and self-reliance, two of the things Nathan had worked his lifetime to achieve.

When Nathan had been a boy, he'd never thought he'd overcome seeing his father shot in the line of duty. He'd had a gregarious dad, a big, boisterous guy who occasionally took Nathan riding in his cruiser. He'd let him work the siren and turn on the lights. It was all in good fun until the day that playtime turned serious. His dad, a highway patrolman, got called to chase a speeder down on the interstate. There hadn't been time to request a replacement or drop off the boy. "Just stay put," his dad had said with a reassuring pat. "Let the old man show you how it's done." He'd secured Nathan's seat belt and taken off with a blast, commandeering the offending vehicle within minutes. Seconds after his dad requested credentials, Nathan witnessed a flash of light streaking from the front seat of that car.

"Is everything okay?" Elizabeth asked from beside him, noting he'd suddenly grown quiet.

"I was just thinking about my dad," he said softly.

"Is it a sad memory?" she asked, reading his expression.

"Yeah, it is."

"I'm sorry, Nathan."

"He was a good guy, you know? Everyone should have a dad like that. I was one lucky kid."

"How old were you when you lost him?"

"Eight."

"That's tough."

"It was, but I pushed past it."

"How?"

"I followed in his footsteps. Became a cop."

"So you could be like he was?"

"But only to a point." He turned to her, emotion clouding in his eyes. "I couldn't do it, Elizabeth. Have a family. People to leave behind."

"So, that's why you've never…?"

He shook his head. "I thought that was it. At least, until now."

He surveyed her as she studied him with kind understanding. This warm, beautiful woman that it had taken him a lifetime to find. "But the real truth is, maybe I was just waiting on the right one." He smiled softly. "Ones. As the case may be."

Elizabeth felt her face warm under his perusal. She wondered if he was really hinting at what she thought he was or whether she was just imagining that he was saying she and Claire could become special to him.

"Life is funny that way. We can never quite foresee some twists of fate."

"Could be we're not meant to."

"I once had a fortune teller offer to read my hand."

"Oh yeah? What did she say?"

Elizabeth shot him a wry smile. "That I didn't want to know."

"Ouch."

"Didn't sound so good to me either."

He studied her a beat as the panorama around them opened up under a clear blue sky.

"We still have some time left. Would you like to hike down to the falls?"

"When you say 'hike down,' do you mean, like, walk on foot?"

He laughed out loud. "This is straight walking all the way. Though I will warn you, the slope's a little steep coming back up."

"Does it require a rope?"

"Not this time."

"I'm in."

Nathan climbed down first so he could help her. "Just back down slowly! Right into my arms!"

Elizabeth realized she wasn't afraid of falling, knowing Nathan would catch her. Besides, the trip went a lot smoother going down than it had going up. Especially without those imaginary wasps to chase her. She had only gone a few feet when she felt his sturdy hands around her waist.

"I've got ya!" he said. "Nice and easy now. You're good."

He lowered her gently to the ground, and once her feet met solid earth, Elizabeth knew she was better than good. Things were absolutely terrific. She could feel him standing behind her, his hands still around her waist as if he regretted the thought of letting her go. He turned her toward him, still holding her in his arms. "How are you doing?"

"Great," she said, nearly breathless. "How about you?"

"Elizabeth, I know this sounds crazy, but I…" He tugged her closer, and she didn't resist. His warmth felt good up against her, tantalizing.

"I know," she said, gazing up at him. "I feel it too."

"You know that thing that you said? About a *once in a lifetime* moment…?"

She nodded as his mouth moved in.

"I think we're having one of those now."

He lowered his mouth toward hers, and she sighed into his kiss, his lips meeting hers with a tender passion. Elizabeth wound her arms around him, and he held her close as he deepened his kisses and they became lost in one another. Elizabeth felt like a woman who'd been wandering in the woods forever. In Nathan's embrace, she was finally finding her way home.

She heard a sharp buzzing sound and snapped her eyes open, the spell suddenly broken.

"What is it?" he asked.

"A wasp!" she cried with alarm. "Buzzing by your shoulder!"

Nathan quickly coiled the rope and packed it away. "We'd better get going. Maybe there *is* a nest around here!"

Elizabeth nodded her agreement, and he took her hand, leading her into the forest. This was by far the grandest adventure Elizabeth had ever had. And it wasn't over yet.

The afternoon only turned more special as she and Nathan approached the base of the falls. They'd hiked for over twenty minutes, and, as Nathan had promised, there'd been no ropes involved. Their trip, however, had been straight down, which meant the return trek was bound to be a killer. "Oh my," Elizabeth proclaimed as dazzling waters cascaded in the sunshine. "It's incredible!" She looked up the high stretch that reached for the clouds. The falls cascaded over an upper ledge. "How did you find this place?"

"Used to come out here exploring. Back when I was first new to Blayton."

"But you haven't been in a while?"

"After a bit, I got busy with the day-to-day. Kind of forgot about it."

"That's hard to believe," she said with an appreciative gasp. "I don't think I ever will."

"I'll never forget it again either," he said, taking her hand. "Not now that I've been here with you."

"Nathan, you…"

He raised her chin with his hand. "What is it?"

"You make me feel something special. Like I'm in the most magical place in the world."

He dove into her eyes with a smile. "I know what you mean."

"Do you think this is going too fast?"

He took her in his arms, then spoke with a husky whisper. "Sometimes I believe it's better not to think at all."

"Those don't sound like the words of a sheriff."

"They're not," he said, bringing his mouth to hers. "They're mine."

Nathan couldn't believe he was letting himself go this way, because he'd simply never experienced it before. But there was something about Elizabeth he found irresistible. Especially as he held her in his arms and the symphony of nature played around them. Birds sang, autumn leaves rustled, and the falls cascaded in glorious rhythm. Pounding again and again, echoing the beat of his heart.

When Perry dropped Claire at home after school, they noticed Elizabeth's SUV wasn't in the drive. "Your mom's not back yet?"

"I thought Nathan was driving, but maybe they met up in town."

Perry glanced over his steering wheel at the neighboring Victorian. "You going to feel safe being here alone?"

"Yeah. Of course!"

"You never hear anything from that place, do you?"

"Other than a couple of rockers creaking in the wind, not really."

"I thought you found Phantom over there."

"We did." She smiled at the memory. "He's such a sweetie too."

"You'll have to introduce us sometime."

Claire's face lit up. "That's right. You haven't met him."

"Some other time, when your mom is home."

"She wouldn't like you being in the house when she's not there," Claire agreed.

"How about on the front porch?"

Elizabeth was so taken by Nathan's embrace, she'd lost all track of the hour. "Oh no!" she said, pushing back in his arms. "What time is it?"

He checked his watch with a frown. "I'm sorry, Elizabeth. It's just past four. I don't know how time got away from me."

"It got away from both of us."

"I can get you back in forty minutes. Faster if we turn on the siren."

"I don't want to do anything reckless."

"I don't either. But if we hustle it up here, we can still make it home safely by five."

"Oh gosh, I hope Claire won't worry."

"I'll radio Martha from the car and have her phone the house."

"Good plan," she said, hastening up the hill. "And, Nathan," she continued as she puffed her way along, "I want to thank you."

"For what?"

"It's been so long. I mean, I've played so many roles. Mother, protector, provider…"

"Then it's good for you to take time out for something else."

She glanced at him, a question in her eyes.

"Being my girl."

Elizabeth cheeks burned fiery hot.

"You don't have to say no. Just take some time to think about it."

"Nathan," she said, pausing a beat. "There's nobody's girl I'd rather be."

He took her hand with a grin. "Want to run?"

"I think I could fly," she said, charging ahead beside him.

Claire carted her guitar onto the porch, where Perry sat waiting with Phantom curled up in his lap. "I think he likes you."

"I think I'm sitting in the sun," Perry replied with a laugh.

"You're always sitting in the sun," Claire said. "You're like the sun, in a way."

"No fair. I'm the one who calls you Sunshine."

"And I'm the one who wrote you a song."

"You?" Perry was visibly moved, slight color appearing at his temples. "What? When?"

"It's a little rough," Claire admitted. "But I've been working on it." She settled down with her guitar and started strumming. "Want to hear it?"

"I'd love to hear it." Perry stroked the cat. "If I can hear above his purring!"

Claire picked out a couple of chords. "Don't laugh now."

"I'd never laugh at you," Perry told her seriously.

She whisked her fingers across the strings a few more times, gradually finding her beat. "Are you ready?" she asked with a grin.

"Any time you are."

"When the leaves start to fall...
Begin fall...alling.
And the winds, autumn winds...
Begin call...alling.
Then I'll be there,
Yeah, be there,

With you
'Neath the blue, blue sky,
No lie.
I'll be there,
I'll be there,
Yeah, with you,
No lie...

Because ba...aby,
I believe,
Yes, I do,
Oh, ba...aby,
I believe,
in you.

And now, I, oh yeah I...
Am fa...alling,
As the winds, autumn winds...
They are call...alling,
And I'm here,
Yes, I'm here,
With you.
'Neath the blue, blue sky,
No lie.
Yes, I'm here,
Yeah, I'm here...
With you.
No lie...

Because ba...aby,
I believe,
Yes, I do,
Oh, ba...aby,
I believe,

in you.

Perry's heart pounded as she set down her guitar. "Claire," he said, meeting her eyes. "That was… Wow. That was, *wow.*"

"Thanks." She blushed faintly. "Like I said, it's still rough."

"There's nothing I'd change about it."

"Really?"

"There's nothing I'd change about you."

Just then, Elizabeth's SUV screeched up the drive, sending gravel flying. She quickly exited and strode toward them. "Honey, I'm so sorry!" she said, obviously out of breath. "Did you get Martha's message?"

"Yeah, I talked to her," Claire said. "It's fine."

Perry stood to meet Mrs. Jennings as she approached, scooting Phantom off his lap.

"I said I'd hang out until you got home. I hope that's okay."

"We didn't go in the house," Claire added quickly.

Elizabeth studied the kids, seeing they'd obviously been sitting on the porch. "Of course, that's fine. Thanks, Perry." She turned to him. "That was nice of you to want to stay with Claire."

"It was honestly no problem." He gazed briefly at Claire. "No problem at all."

Chapter Eight

Melody met the others behind the Fenton house at nine o'clock. They'd ridden their bicycles there through the shadows and now huddled together by the back door with their backpacks. A third-quarter moon hung high in the October sky, reflecting eerily in the house's windows. Somewhere off in the distance, a hoot owl called.

"This is creepy," Joy said in a whisper.

"Way creepy," Lilly agreed.

"Don't be such babies," Penelope scolded. "I could have done all this myself."

Melody briefly considered taking her up on it. "Here," she said, handing her backpack over and calling Penelope's bluff.

Penelope narrowed her eyes in the darkness. "What's this?"

"You said you wanted to do it alone."

Penelope hesitated, glancing at the others. "There's too much to do for just one person."

"Fine," Melody said. She tried the knob to the back door, finding it locked, then stared at Joy with agitation. "You were supposed to crawl in through the basement window and unlock it."

Joy's color deepened a shade. "I *did* come by today, but…"

"But what?"

She hung her head, then spoke softly. "I didn't fit."

Penelope started to laugh, but Melody's glare stopped her. "You probably wouldn't either."

Penelope glanced down at her own curvy figure. At fifteen, all the girls had developed, some of them in greater proportions than others. And each was a little on the heavy side, excepting Melody. All eyes turned on her.

"You want me to go in there? Now? *Alone?*"

Melody's pulse quickened.

"You're the only one who fits," Lilly said.

"Guess this is one time being skinny pays off," Penelope said.

If this was the payoff, Melody wasn't sure she wanted to win this lotto. "Maybe we should just wait. Until closer to Halloween, like Joy said."

"But we're already here," Lilly protested.

"Yeah," Penelope chimed in. "Here with all the stuff."

Stuff like a bunch of cheap bed sheets, rope, and party balloons they could blow up and shove under the sheets to look like ghost heads. It had all seemed such a great plan. They'd set up the house with a bunch of fake goblins peering out the windows and throw stones and make noises until they were sure the Jennings were awake. Then they'd run for the hills like scared rabbits.

Melody peered around the corner of the house at the graveyard. No wait, they'd better run in the other direction. She'd hoped Joy would back her up in putting this whole thing off. Instead, the other girl handed her a flashlight. "You can take this."

Melody puffed out a breath. "Thanks, Joy."

Melody dumped her backpack on a step and went around to the basement window. It was always a little loose and had a lock that had been broken off years ago. She jimmied it open and stared inside at the cavernous black basement. It smelled of dampness, mold, and who knew what else that could have been down there fermenting forever.

"If you see old Mrs. Fenton's corpse, step over it," Penelope added unhelpfully from nearby.

"Thanks, Penny. Appreciate it."

Getting down on her belly, Melody extended her legs over the window's ledge and draped them inside. The thought flashed through her brain that something sinister might grab them. But she willed that thought away and slid her torso in next. With her grip on the ledge, she drew a breath and dropped down to the floor. Standing up on her tiptoes, she could just reach the flashlight Joy extended toward her. "Be careful!" Joy whispered.

"And hurry!" the others said.

Like I really want to take my time with this…

Her toe hit something that scraped across concrete and sent her tripping forward. Melody righted herself with a start. She checked the floor with the flashlight, seeing she'd just kicked a tin watering can.

"Shhh!" Penelope called from above.

"Why don't you shut up and come do it?" Melody hissed back. She wasn't even sure why she was here. As long as a few days ago, she'd decided she no longer wanted in on this game. It wasn't right picking on Claire the way they all did. Melody realized she was the one who had started it. But after a point, wasn't enough *enough*?

She found the stairs and followed them up to the kitchen, one creaky footfall at a time. Each time a new board shrieked, Melody shivered. It was as if this whole house was sending her a warning. A warning about what she ought not to do. Skittering noises sounded from across the room, and she wheeled her light in that direction, finding a passel of field mice. They were picking at straw from an old bale of hay that had been left rotting in the corner. Melody didn't know why old man Robeson hadn't cleaned this place up. He was angling to sell it after all. Then she remembered he'd had the lawn reseeded in September. The hay was probably left over from that. She could hear the other girls whispering outside, but as she climbed higher, their voices faded in the night.

Melody swallowed hard, thinking this was a stupid idea. Totally lame. But she had nobody to blame for it but herself. If she could wind back time, she'd undo everything. Maybe even make nice with Claire from the start. She'd been new in Blayton once herself and understood how awkward it was feeling like an outsider. While she acted tough on the surface, the truth was Melody was secretly ashamed of the bully she'd become. That wasn't a person her mom could be proud of, or her Uncle Nathan either. And that wasn't who Melody really wanted to be. At times, she'd thought it was too late to change things. She had her bad-girl reputation to uphold, after all. Then again, if she wanted to change, she'd have to do right. Not keep on hedging down a dark path.

Finally reaching the kitchen, she pressed open the door and stepped into the chilly house. It was even colder in here than in the basement, owing to the fact that the heat was turned off. Melody thought she remembered learning something in science class about warm air rising but dismissed her rationalizing. What did it matter how cold it was where? All she needed to do was get to the back door and let the others in. Or maybe she could meet them, then stop this! Yeah. Nothing had been done yet. It wasn't really too late. What was it her Uncle Nathan always said? *Actions speak louder than words.* So what if she and her friends had schemed to do something nasty? If it never came off, it would be like they'd never planned it at all.

But the only way to stop things involved getting to the outside door. That meant passing through Mrs. Fenton's room. In her dying days, she'd been kept in the dining room because she'd been too weak to climb the stairs. The table had been taken out, and her hospice bed had been wheeled in. Only one piece of dining room furniture remained.

Melody turned toward the threshold to that room, her heart pounding. She knew the mahogany sideboard with its matching antique mirror stood there still. There were rumors about that old mirror. Stories she and the other kids joked about but that nobody thought were real. If you passed by it under a full moon, you could see the face of a ghost in the glass. Mrs. Fenton's ghost, most likely. Though nobody knew for sure, as no one had been brave enough to test the theory. Melody hurried into the room, reminding herself that a full moon was a whole week away. She had nothing to worry about now. It was just a dumb superstition.

She was halfway across the room when something stopped her. Through the back door windowpane, she could see the others hunkered together waiting to be let in. But here in the blackness of this room, she felt a presence. It was something she didn't totally understand, but still felt she knew. Melody swept the parameters of the room with her flashlight, its low beam bouncing off the surrounding windows. Then suddenly, her light went out. She shook the flashlight and batteries rattled inside it, but it failed to switch back on.

"Melody!" She could hear Joy's hoarse whisper from beyond the door. "Come on!"

She wanted to go toward them. Really she did. But it was as if magnets were attached to her eyes, pulling them toward the mirror. Melody heard heavy breathing, then realized it was her own as her heart *thump-thumped, thump-thumped* in her ears. Her gaze panned slowly to the sideboard, then gradually...oh so gradually...to its dusty, overhanging mirror. Melody stared straight ahead, her jaw unhinged. And in that moment, she knew.

"*Holy crap!*" she shrieked, racing for the back door and bolting through it.

Joy caught her arm, but she broke free. "Melody! What's wrong?"

Lights in the Jennings house next door flipped on.

"Let's get going," Penelope urged, strapping on her backpack.

Lilly and Joy hopped on their bikes.

"Where's Melody?" Penelope asked.

Joy pointed down the road about a hundred yards to where Melody was already riding away, pedaling fast.

Nathan and Bernie went through the Fenton house in detail but didn't find a thing, other than the basement window pushed open and the back door left ajar. Once Nathan was satisfied there was nothing more, he sent his deputy home. Then he went to speak with the woman who'd placed the 9-1-1 call.

Elizabeth opened her front door wearing pajama pants and a sweatshirt, her shoulder-length hair pulled back in a ponytail. There was worry in her deep brown eyes, and it pained Nathan to see it. If there was a way on earth to keep her from worrying ever again, he'd ensure it.

"It's okay," he told her. "The place is clear."

She breathed a sigh, but her brow still wrinkled in concern. "We heard something, I swear. It sounded just like a woman screaming."

"I'm not saying you imagined it," he assured her. "It could have been anything. The wind, a fox…"

"It definitely wasn't the wind," Elizabeth said. "And how on earth could a fox get that back door open?"

Nathan wasn't sure but didn't want to trouble her further. "The important thing is, there's nobody in there now. Bernie and I scoured the place from top to bottom."

He spied Claire standing at the base of the stairs, the same worried look on her face as on her mother's.

"It's okay," he told her. "Whatever it was, it's gone now."

The teen wrapped her arms around herself in a shiver. "It sounded really weird. Like, I don't know. It wasn't even from this world."

"Everything sounds different at night," Nathan promised. "It could even have been a cat."

As if on cue, Phantom appeared from the kitchen.

"But this cat's been right here all night long," Claire said.

Nathan glanced from one to the other, sensing their level of concern. Of course they'd been bothered by whatever had occurred next door. While he couldn't explain it, he was sure Elizabeth and her girl had heard *something.* And, whatever it was had left both of them spooked.

"Tell you what," he said kindly. "If it makes you feel any better, I can stay here tonight."

"Here?" Elizabeth asked with alarm.

"I'll sleep on the sofa."

"Can he, Mom? Please?"

Elizabeth studied her daughter, then glanced at Nathan. "Are you sure?"

"I'm happy to do it. I don't really suspect any more funny business will go on next door, but I'm glad to provide backup just in case."

The tension in Elizabeth's expression eased. "That really *is* beyond the call."

"No, it's not."

"He's insisting, Mom."

Elizabeth pursed her lips for a beat. "You're really nice to do this."

"Got a pillow and a blanket?" Nathan asked her.

The next afternoon, Belle stunned Nathan by walking into his office.

"This is a nice surprise." He stood to greet her, but something in her demeanor gave him pause. "Belle? What is it?"

"Nathan, I don't want you to get excited now…"

There was no more surefire way to set his nerves on edge. *What is going on here?*

"But I came to tell you Melody and I are leaving town."

"*Leaving?*"

"This may seem sudden—"

"Damn straight it does." He took his sister by the shoulders. "Where on earth is this coming from?"

She met his eyes in a determined fashion. "I'm not asking you to talk me out of it. I want you to understand."

Nathan released his grip, his head still reeling. "Understand *what?*"

There was a peaceful calm about her. "Just that it's time. Melody's decided she's ready to go home."

"Back to Bristol? But you said you'd never—"

"It's not like we're going away forever. We'll still be in touch."

"But why now? So all of a sudden?"

"It's been building for a while," she told him. "This change in Melody. She's ready now to face a lot of things."

"I think I'd like to hear that from her myself."

Belle glanced toward the door, where Melody had appeared in the threshold.

"Uncle Nathan," she said, rushing toward him. "I'm going to miss you."

She wrapped her arms around him in a hug, and a lump welled in Nathan's throat. "You too, kiddo. You too."

He met his sister's eyes.

"Are you sure?"

An hour later, Dan hugged Belle good-bye at the orchard.

"I didn't think our date went that bad," he said, choking back his emotion.

"It didn't," she said. She met his gaze. "It was wonderful."

"If only there could be another time."

"There will be."

"You sound so sure."

A smile tilted up the edges of her mouth. "Maybe I know something you don't."

"Maybe."

"Don't lose faith."

"It's hard."

"I know."

"When will I see you?"

"Soon."

"Promise?"

She wrapped her arms around him and did what Dan had only dreamed of. She kissed him on the lips. "Does that feel like a promise to you?"

Claire walked in the door, appearing troubled.

"Hey, hon," Elizabeth said. "How was school today?"

"Okay."

She continued to read her daughter's expression but couldn't decipher it. "Okay?"

Claire dropped her backpack to the floor and slunk down on the sofa, studying the worn hook rug.

"Claire?"

Her eyes were moist. "Something weird is going on, Mom."

"Something weird, how?"

"I'm not sure. It's just a feeling."

"Did something happen today?"

"Not really. It's just that…"

"What?"

"Melody wasn't in school."

"Maybe she was sick."

"Perry heard she moved."

"What?" Elizabeth asked in shock. "Just like that?"

"Yeah."

"Wow. Nathan didn't say a thing. I mean she *is* his sister. He might have mentioned—"

"Perry says that happens here."

"What happens?"

"People disappear. All of a sudden."

"Now, that's silly, Claire."

"I know it sounds weird, but Perry says—"

Elizabeth sat beside her daughter. "Look, I don't want you getting yourself worked up over some circulating high school rumors. Let me ask Nathan about it, all right? I'm sure he'll give me the straight story."

"Yeah?"

"Yeah."

Elizabeth opened her arms for a hug. "Now, come here."

Claire scooted toward her, and she drew her into her arms. "Whatever's going on, I'm sure there's some logical explanation. Okay?"

"Okay," Claire said, hugging her back.

But the tightness of her embrace told Elizabeth her daughter was afraid.

The only thing she didn't know was *of what?*

Nathan paced the well-worn path between his desk and the coffeepot, unable to get back to work. He couldn't shake the feeling that something was wrong. It wasn't like his sister to make snap decisions. Then again, Belle was fairly headstrong. Once she was determined to do something, there was no talking her out of it. Like the time she moved to Blayton, for instance. It had taken Nathan a while to find out about it. He hadn't known until after his two-year trek out west. Nathan was ashamed of the guy he'd been then. Someone so into sorting out his own head, he hadn't kept up with his family. He hadn't even known Belle and Tony were having trouble. Not that Belle would have entrusted him with that knowledge at the time. She and Nathan had only gotten close after he'd tracked her down in Blayton. The town was recruiting a new sheriff, and, with his outdoorsy know-how and previous police experience, Nathan was an ideal candidate for the job. He liked it here, so decided to stay. Plus, his priorities had changed. He'd come to realize his role in looking after other people was actually the best way to honor himself. It helped him become the sort of man he'd always wanted to be. Someone like his father.

"Something troubling you, Sheriff?" Martha's eyes were just visible above the top of her book.

Yeah, something was bothering him all right. Something that had to do with his sister's sudden move. He checked the clock against his watch, seeing it was just past five o'clock. Most nights he worked until six. But tonight wouldn't be one of them. He strode back to his office and nabbed his keys off his desk. "I'm going to knock off early," he told her.

She set down her book and studied him.

"Is everything all right with Belle? Did something happen when she and Melody stopped by earlier?"

"I'll let you know," he said, heading out the door.

By the time Nathan got to Belle's house, the interior lights were all off and the doors were locked tight. "Well, I'll be…" He couldn't believe they'd packed up and gone this quickly. He peered through a first-floor window and saw the furniture still in place. Then again, that wasn't unusual. Most places in Blayton were rented fully furnished, and Belle's house was no exception.

He strolled around to the screen porch out back and stepped through it toward the kitchen. Through the windowpanes in the door, he could see inside. Normally, Belle kept a bunch of junk on the refrigerator: magnets, Melody's school pictures, reminder notices for events at the library. Now the front of the refrigerator was bare, gleaming in the pale light streaming in through the kitchen windows. She and Melody had gone, all right. *Poof!* Just like a puff of air.

Nathan kicked himself now for not getting Belle's new address in Bristol, if she'd even gotten one on such short notice. He should have asked her what they planned to do. Stay with friends? Hold up temporarily in a hotel? And why now? Right after the start of the school year, when surely it would have been better to at least wait until winter break?

These and a million other questions were occurring to him now, but he'd been so broadsided by Belle's surprise visit, he hadn't thought to ask them then. Nathan sat heavily on a bench and rested his elbows on the old picnic table that stood on the back porch. He'd have to find them somehow. Maybe he could enlist Bernie's help. Sure wouldn't hurt things if their communications systems got back up and rolling. He'd give Lex a call tomorrow to check on the status of things.

Chapter Nine

Elizabeth and Nathan sat her kitchen table drinking coffee.

"Thanks for being here tonight."

"Claire's first high school dance." He sipped from his mug. "It's a big deal."

Elizabeth loved the way Nathan *got* everything. He was so intuitive, always sensing what she and Claire needed before even they could see it themselves. Like a few nights before when there'd been that disruption next door. Elizabeth never would have imposed on Nathan by asking him to stay. But he'd understood she and Claire would be more comfortable if he did. So when he'd offered, it had seemed only gracious to accept. The truth was, Elizabeth had rested easier with a man in the house. Especially a man with gorgeous hazel eyes who filled out a uniform the way Nathan did. His hat sat on the table beside his elbow. He'd be stopping by the dance later just to check on things, though Bernie was the main man on duty there tonight.

Claire appeared in the threshold, an utter transformation. Her bangs were pinned back and her face brushed with the slightest hint of makeup.

"You look very nice," Nathan said. "That Perry is a lucky guy."

Claire blushed and did a slight pirouette in her short pastel dress. Its color was light pumpkin spice, ideal for the season. It had actually belonged to Elizabeth, but she'd only worn it once to a press dinner in Richmond. She was surprised it fit her daughter so well. Claire really was growing up. "You're beautiful, Claire."

"Thanks."

The doorbell rang, and Nathan stood. "Want me to get that?"

"Please," Elizabeth answered.

When he'd gone, she gave her daughter a hug. "I want you to have fun tonight. But not *too much* fun."

"Mo-om." Claire sighed heavily. "Next you're going to tell me to 'make smart choices.'"

"That's not a bad idea."

Nathan pulled back the door and let Perry inside. Aw, nice. The kid was all dressed up in a jacket and tie and— good for him—carrying a corsage. "Perry," he said with a nod, "you clean up well."

Perry firmly shook his hand, man-to-man like. "Thanks, sir."

"Claire's with her mom in the kitchen."

Perry started to head that way, but Nathan stopped him. "Um, son, I want you to drive carefully tonight."

"Yes, sir, of course."

"And no *loitering* between here and the school, if you know what I'm saying."

Perry shifted on his feet. "I really like Claire a lot. I'm not going to do anything stupid."

"I didn't imagine you would." He met the boy's eyes. "Which is why I'll be stopping by the dance later to check on you."

Perry just stared at him like a deer caught in somebody's headlights.

Nathan swatted his shoulder with a grin. "You two have fun now."

A few minutes later, Elizabeth and Nathan stood on the front porch, waving the kids good-bye. In spite of herself, Elizabeth felt the sting of moisture in her eyes.

"They'll be okay, you know," Nathan told her.

"I know. It's just that…"

"Yeah, it's hard seeing them grow up. Hard but good at the same time."

"Yes."

"Elizabeth," he said, turning to her. "That's what you want, for Claire to find her own way."

She nodded and wiped back her tears. "I know this is stupid."

He brought his arms around her. "No, it's not."

She shared a shaky smile. "What makes you so right about everything?"

"I'm the sheriff."

"Go on!"

"Plus…" He tightened his embrace. "I've got some special inside knowledge on Claire."

"How so?"

He brought his forehead to hers. When he spoke, his voice was husky. "I'm developing a thing for her mother." He was near enough to kiss her now, his mouth hovering over hers.

"Let's go inside," Elizabeth said, nearly breathless.

She walked toward the kitchen, her knees trembling, and her skin on fire. She'd never wanted a man like she wanted Nathan. There was something so special about him. Just being in his arms felt like heaven. And when he kissed her, *oh my…*

Nathan walked up behind her where she stood by the coffeepot.

"Want some more coffee?"

His voice was a whisper beside her. "No."

The next thing she knew, his lips were against her nape, and Elizabeth felt faint, dizzy from the sheer pleasure of his kiss. "Nathan," she breathed, gripping the counter for support. "I…"

He spun her gently in his arms and tilted her chin up toward his. "Yes?"

She was lost in his eyes and the deep longing she saw there. "I…don't know what to do."

"Then let me lead."

He brought his mouth to hers, and Elizabeth shut her eyes, thinking this must be a dream. Nothing this wonderful had ever happened to her. He pulled her to him and kissed her more deeply and with even more ardor than he'd exhibited outdoors. Parts of her anatomy came alive that she'd forgotten existed, and now all of her was calling to be cuddled and caressed by him. His hands trailed down her back and settled lower as he pressed the lower half of his body to hers. The rock-hard lower part of his body. "Elizabeth," he said between kisses, "if I were a reckless man…"

"But you're not," she whispered back.

A sound escaped him that was half moan, half growl. "God, woman, you're driving me insane."

"Then we should stop."

"Yes."

When he pulled back, his hair was mussed and his complexion ruddy. "I'm sorry, I—"

"No. It was both of us."

"We can't—"

"Not with Claire."

"We have to set the example."

"Yes."

She stared up at this gorgeous man, wondering how she'd been fortunate enough find him. His gaze poured over her, and she felt warm from head to toe.

"You're wonderful. Do you know that? Hands down the most incredible woman I've ever met."

"I believe that's the nicest thing a man has ever told me."

"Then you'd better get used to it. Because I'm going to be telling you again…" He brought his lips to hers, chastely this time. "And again…"

How she wanted him to carry her away. Straight to her bedroom upstairs. But this wasn't the right time or the right way. Both of them knew it. "And you," she said between soft kisses, "are without a doubt the sexiest guy I've ever had occasion to kiss."

"I'll take that as a compliment," he said, kissing her once more.

An hour later, he finished his iced coffee and placed his hat on his head. "I'll be back before you know it."

"Want me to come with you?" Elizabeth offered.

"Don't you think it puts enough pressure on the kids having me show up?"

Elizabeth laughed sweetly. "You're right."

She was beautiful standing there, her lips and cheeks still bright with color from all that kissing. And man, didn't he want to kiss her again. He could make an occupation of it. Nathan didn't know how he was lucky enough to have a woman like Elizabeth come into his life. It was like that old saying about things happening when you weren't expecting them.

And the cool thing was, he'd gotten another person in the deal. Claire was a good kid with a big heart and a lot of love and admiration for her mother. That part was obvious, which only made Nathan like her all the more. He felt glad he'd been able to contribute in some small way. Although they were new in town and he was still getting to know them, Nathan couldn't fight the uncanny feeling that he and Elizabeth and Claire somehow *fit* together.

"Shouldn't take more than an hour," he said, strapping on his holster.

"I'll keep the home fires burning."

He shot her a wink as he walked out the door. "I like the way you said that."

Meanwhile, at the dance, Perry refilled Claire's cup from the punch bowl. The place was all decorated like Halloween, with glowing plastic jack-o'-lanterns on the tables and everything. "Thanks," she said, holding her heels in one hand. She'd kicked them off about midway through the first number and had been dancing barefoot on the gym floor ever since. "I'm really thirsty."

"No wonder." Perry laughed. "Who knew a girl could move so fast?"

"It was fast dancing."

"Yeah." He handed her the cup. "Wonder when they'll start playing the slow ones?" His gaze travelled across the room to a bunch of girls seated at a table. A couple of them stood and headed in their direction. "Uh-oh, don't look now, but we've got company."

Before they could move away, Lilly and Joy approached. At first, Claire thought they'd ignore her, but Joy walked right up to her instead.

Claire took a quick sip, unsure of what to say. "Punch is good."

"I'll get some," Joy said, "but first…" Her expression was slightly downcast. "I wanted to apologize."

"What?"

"We both do," Lilly said beside her.

"For what?"

Joy shrugged and hung her head. But Claire knew. They'd been behind the whole locker thing and likely other schemes too. Who knew what else might have come off had Melody stayed in town.

"It's cool," Claire told them.

Relief flooded their faces. "Really?" Joy asked.

"Really."

Lilly cocked her head to the side. "Just like that? Wow," she said to Joy, "she's pretty chill."

Perry drew closer and draped his arm over Claire's shoulder. "It's nice to see everybody getting in the holiday spirit."

"It's Halloween, Perry," Joy said, appearing puzzled.

"Even *ghosts* can be nice," he said.

"Yeah, well, we wouldn't know." She glanced at her friend. "Would we, Lilly?"

Lilly looked vacant. "About...?"

"Never mind." Joy nudged her arm. "Come on, let's go."

"Aren't we going to get some punch?"

"You all have fun now!" Perry waved goodbye, angling Claire away.

She giggled, still tucked under his arm. "Can you believe that?"

"Think it's 'cause Melody's gone?"

"I don't know. Somehow..."

"Somehow what?"

"Somehow I didn't get the feeling Melody was really that bad. Underneath, I mean. You know what I'm saying?"

"I know what you're saying exactly."

Just then the music changed to a much slower tempo, and the dance floor cleared. Perry took Claire's cup and set it aside. "Want to?"

She glanced around, noting only a few other couples dancing. Serious couples. Ones that everybody in the school knew were going together. Although Perry hadn't asked her to be his girlfriend yet, if he did, she knew she would say yes. "All right."

He took her by the hand and led her to the center of the room, just below where a retro disco ball sparkled, sending shimmers of colored light across the dance floor. It was awkward at first, and Claire didn't know where to put her hands. On his shoulders? Around his waist? She gave a few false starts, then burst out laughing. "I'm sorry, I haven't really done this before."

He stared at her in disbelief. "Slow dance with a guy?"

She shyly shook her head.

He smiled warmly. "It's okay. Just give me a hug."

"What?"

"Here," he said, stepping toward her.

He settled her arms up over his shoulders so she could link her hands behind his neck, then wound his arms around her middle. She'd never been so close to a boy. Ultra close. And warm. And Perry smelled so good, like he was wearing aftershave or something. "This all right?"

"Six inches!" Bernie cut in.

Perry turned toward the deputy, who'd suddenly appeared at their side with a flashlight. "Huh?"

"Six inches," Bernie repeated. "That's the distance you're supposed to keep between you."

Claire felt her face color.

Perry stared at him with pleading eyes. "Come on, man. It's our first dance."

"Let's not make it be your last."

Perry raised his eyebrows at Claire, and she suppressed a giggle.

"Yes, sir. No problem, sir. Don't want any worries with the law." He stepped back a pace, making more space between them. Bernie clucked with satisfaction, then strolled away, muttering something about *kids these days.*

"Don't worry," Perry whispered to her. "He'll go out for a smoke break any minute."

"How do you know?"

"I've been watching him. He leaves every fifteen minutes or so, then comes back in smelling like a chimney."

"Is he hiding it?"

"Doesn't want Janet to know. She says it'll kill him someday."

"Well, it might."

"Yeah, well, that's Bernie's business."

"I suppose."

"See? There. He's leaving."

Claire peered past Perry's shoulder and saw he was right. Bernie glanced quickly around, then slipped out the gym's side door. "Poor guy," she said in sympathy.

"Lucky me," Perry said, holding her tight.

Claire hadn't really known what dancing was until this moment with Perry. Now she saw why couples did it in all those romantic movies. It was the most awesome thing in the world. Almost as awesome as that moment on the sofa when Perry had kissed her. It had just been on the cheek but set her whole world on fire. If he ever got around to her lips, Claire wasn't sure she could stand the combustion.

Nathan passed Bernie when he was headed inside. "How are things going in there?"

"No troubles so far." Bernie held his hand to the side, trying to conceal his cigarette. But gray puffs of smoke swirled skyward in the night.

"I thought you were giving that up."

"I'm trying, man. But sometimes it's hard."

Nathan scrutinized his face, surmising something. Bernie rarely got stressed, unless it was his wife that was stressing him. "You and Janet have a fight?"

Bernie took a drag on his cigarette and hung his head. "All I did was make a comment about that stupid magazine."

"What magazine?"

"*Pet Psychic*."

Nathan resisted a grin. "I see."

"I only asked how pets could be psychic? I mean, how can anyone know?" Bernie dropped his butt to the ground and crushed it out. "Then she started fuming about how it wasn't the *pets* that were psychic, but the people who communed with them."

"Doesn't sound like there was an easy way out of that one."

"No."

"Why don't you take her some flowers? Make it up to her?"

"Me? But I didn't do anything wrong!"

Nathan studied the butt on the ground. "Better than pushing up daisies, my friend."

"You know I'm trying to quit."

"Don't let a temporary setback stop you. Just jump back on that wagon, pal." He held out his palm and waited until Bernie reluctantly extracted his pack. He slapped it into Nathan's hand with a weighty sigh. "Thanks, Nathan."

"Any time."

Bernie scratched his head, thinking.

"Know where I can get flowers at this hour?"

"They sell them at Evan's, but they lock up at nine."

Bernie shot him an urgent stare.

"Go on," Nathan said with a laugh. "I'll hold down the fort here."

"Are you sure?"

"The store's just around the corner."

"It'll sure beat sleeping on the sofa tonight."

"And don't speed!" Nathan called after him as he raced for his car.

When Nathan entered the gym, he encountered the typical scene. Couples crowded onto the dance floor under the disco ball and groups of teacher chaperones standing around gabbing rather than paying attention. Not that there was too much to worry about with this group. These were mostly good kids, and even the gnarly ones had their merits. It wasn't easy being in high school sometimes. Nathan was sure Claire could attest to that. He scanned the room searching for her, then finally spotted her on the dance floor—*wouldn't you know it?*—snuggled right up in Perry's arms.

A slow song must have just ended, because the different couples were splitting apart, but not Claire and Perry. They just stood there gazing at each other like two love-struck kids. *Uh-oh, here it comes.* Perry was leaning forward and Claire was tilting her face toward his. Nathan could try to stop it, but that wouldn't be fair. He might not even have been here had he chatted with Bernie a moment further. Perry brought his mouth to Claire's, and then, in the blink of an eye, it was over. Both of them backed away like they'd frightened themselves silly. Nathan chuckled to himself, remembering what it was like being young. Lately, he'd been feeling fairly youthful himself.

He was standing by the punch bowl when Claire and Perry returned to it.

"Nathan!" she said, her cheeks bright pink. "I didn't know you were here."

If she appeared surprised, Perry looked positively petrified. "When did you come in?"

"A few minutes ago."

Claire's eyes registered panic.

"You won't tell Mom?"

"I figure that's your business."

Perry sighed audibly. "Thanks."

Nathan glanced around the room at the others. "Looks like folks are having fun."

"Yeah, mostly." Perry watched a girl race for the bathroom in tears. Another one scurried after her, carrying tissues for comfort. "Somebody always breaks up at these things."

"Doesn't seem the best place to do it," Nathan observed.

"Uh-uh," Claire agreed.

"Well, I'm going to circulate a bit and talk to some teachers. You kids have fun." But before he walked away, he pointed his finger at Perry. "But not too much."

Claire helped herself to more punch as Nathan walked away. "He's really pretty cool."

"Yeah. Everybody likes him."

"I think Mom likes him."

Perry's face brightened. "Yeah?"

"Yeah."

Perry watched Nathan moving from one group of grown-ups to another, sharing pleasantries. "Does he like her back?"

"Oh…yeah." Claire said, drawing out the words.

Perry clinked his punch cup to hers. "That's sweet."

When Nathan returned to Elizabeth's, it was nearly ten o'clock. "I'm sorry," he told her. "Took a little longer than I thought. Bernie needed a favor."

"Everything all right?" she asked.

"Yeah." He removed his hat and set it on the kitchen table. "The dance was going well too."

"Did you see Claire and Perry?"

"Uh-huh," he said with a mysterious smile.

"What's that supposed to mean? Nathan…?"

"Just that they're getting close."

"Close?"

"Mind if I have a glass of water?"

"Sure." She prepared one and brought it to him. "I think you'd better define *close*."

"I think you'd better ask your daughter."

"Nothing happen—?"

"Nothing bad."

"But—"

He drained his glass, then put it down. "Ask Claire."

She folded her arms and studied him as he removed his holster and set it aside. "Hmm."

"Hmm, what?"

"I'd hate to think you're keeping secrets from me."

"What if she asked me not to tell?"

"Did she?"

"You're being very tricky with this. I should put you on my interrogation team."

She laughed lightly. "You don't have an interrogation team."

"Sure I do." His eyes sparkled. "But it's just me and Bernie."

She playfully shoved his arm. "What I am going to do with you?"

"Keep me?" He raised his brow. "At least until you find someone better."

"I don't think I could find anyone better."

"Then kiss me, Elizabeth." He took her in his arms. "Kiss me like you mean that."

"But the kids?"

He lowered his lips toward hers.

"Won't be home for another hour."

"You're very hard to resist."

He closed the distance between them.

"Good."

By the time Perry brought Claire home, Nathan had gone. Elizabeth politely waited inside rather than rushing to the door, to give them some privacy saying good night. Nathan had suggested she do that, and he was right. But it was awfully hard to hide in the kitchen when she knew her baby girl might be getting her first good-night kiss.

Elizabeth felt like a teenager herself. She and Nathan had practically made out all night. She'd never been so attracted to a man, and for all the right reasons. Nathan was handsome, sexy, intelligent, and kind. And he kissed like some kind of sex god. Elizabeth went a bit light-headed just at the thought. There were so many wonderful memories she and Nathan were already starting to build. She had fun with him. What's more, she trusted him. Trusted him to be the stand-up sort of guy who stuck around for the long haul. Elizabeth caught her breath, wondering if she was getting ahead of herself. Envisioning a future with Nathan. But it was impossible not to when he was so impossibly wonderful to be around.

She heard the front door close and soon Claire entered the kitchen, looking happy.

"How did everything go?"

"Good," Claire said. Her expression was pleasant, but it appeared she was floating somewhere, like off in the clouds.

"Just good?"

"Real good." She sighed, then turned her eyes on her mom's. "How was your night?"

Elizabeth casually flipped back her hair. "Good."

Claire cracked a smile. "Good, Mom?"

Elizabeth sighed giddily. "Real good."

Then they both laughed and hugged each other, and said they were oh so tired but would talk more in the morning. Privately, though, both of them knew there was only so much the other would share. And that was okay.

Chapter Ten

Elizabeth went to her newspaper office on Monday determined to make lemons into lemonade. If she didn't have Internet this morning—and she doubted she would—she'd get going on her plans for that first edition anyway. Didn't folks used to write news before Wi-Fi? Of course they did. Elizabeth could do it too. She'd start the old-fashioned way. Longhand and in person. She'd thought up the idea of interviewing the townspeople and showcasing some local color. She could type up her notes into stories and prepare the periodical's layout in her software program. She'd add a few interesting photos and...tah-dahhh! She'd have a first edition. She might even get someone at the camera shop to help her print out hard copies. That way, she'd have something concrete to show for herself if the electronic version took longer due to technical difficulties. She still hadn't been able to reach Jerry and was becoming increasingly frustrated on that account. She'd even tried his administrative assistant's number, but had only achieved the same bad results.

She was glad Claire had such a fun weekend. She'd had a pretty glorious one too. Nathan had promised to drop in today to check on her Internet and see how she was doing. She was just making up a list of potential interview candidates when he walked in the door.

"How are things?" he asked with a grin that set her tailbone tingling.

"Coming along."

He tipped his hat in her direction and studied her a moment. When he spoke, his voice was husky. "I missed seeing you yesterday."

Elizabeth's heart fluttered. "We can't possibly see each other all the time."

"I'll have to check the law books and see if that's written in somewhere." He strode toward her and kissed the top of her head. "But I doubt it."

Her gaze shot to the front window. "Nathan!" she protested, laughing. "Someone will see us!"

"Just smoothing your hair down a bit," he said in a playful growl, "with my lips."

Heat streaked to her nether regions, which had no business being *heated* at this early hour. She set her papers aside and stood, collecting herself. "Not too busy this morning?"

"Oh yeah, there's plenty to do. Today I make my rounds and do security checks."

"Security checks?"

"Of local area businesses. Ensure locks are in working order, smoke detectors are functioning, that sort of thing." As if to demonstrate, he walked to the front window and attempted to raise its sash. Despite the fact that it was locked, he jimmied it open after a few short tries. "Just what I suspected. This old catch has gone bad. I'll send somebody by to replace it."

"I'm not sure if now's the best time," Elizabeth hedged. "I'm still out of touch with Richmond and haven't gotten my budget money for next month."

He slowly stroked his chin and appraised the window. "No worries," he said after a beat. "I know a guy who won't charge much."

Before she could argue further, he turned to question her. "What've you got planned for today?"

She smiled with newfound confidence. "I thought I'd start interviewing. No sense letting time go to waste when I can be roughing out my first edition."

"That's my girl." His eyes sparkled with admiration, and Elizabeth felt warmed through and through. "I knew you'd find a work-around."

"Work-around?"

"To this temporary Internet setback." He glanced over at the router. "I'm assuming still no dice?"

She shook her head.

"We're not having any better luck at the station."

"What if we get hit by a crime wave?"

"Unlikely." He briefly removed his hat to run a hand through his short brown hair. "In the five years I've been here, haven't had to throw anyone in the pokey yet."

"I guess that's something to be grateful for."

"You got that straight."

"Have you learned anything more about Belle and Melody?" she asked him.

"Only that Belle talked to Dan before she left." He blew out a breath. "That sister of mine... When she gets something in her head, I guess she's going to do it. I only wish she'd given me more warning, or at least a forwarding address."

"I'm sure she'll send one."

"Yeah, I know you're right. Once she settles in."

Elizabeth watched him with understanding. "I know you're going to miss her."

He appeared sad a moment, then replaced his hat.

"Well, like she said, it's not like she's gone forever. We'll be back in touch."

"I'm sure you will. Your sister and niece love you very much."

"How do you know that?"

"How could they not?" she asked matter-of-factly.

"Ah, Elizabeth, you're such a sweetheart." He surreptitiously glanced out the window, then—seeing no one—gave her a quick peck on the lips. "Dinner later?" he asked in a whisper.

Her face flushed. "Where?"

"Your place."

"What?"

"That's how you're going to repay me for fixing that window," he said with a wink. "And anything else around here that needs doing."

To Elizabeth's surprise, there was way more that *needed doing* in that old newspaper shop than she imagined. Apart from the window lock being broken, the smoke detector was not just out of batteries, its insides were rusted through. So it had to be replaced completely. As did the dead bolt on the back door that apparently hadn't worked well in years. While Nathan took care of things there, Elizabeth interviewed Janet first, then headed out to the orchard to speak with Dan and take photos of the fall colors. When she returned hours later, Nathan was still hard at work. He'd removed his uniform shirt, holster, and hat, and crouched by the back door with an electric screwdriver, wearing nothing but an undershirt and his slacks. He turned toward her, and musculature rippled across his back. "Almost done here."

"I can't thank you enough." Elizabeth glanced around at the improvements. "I really didn't mean to put you out this way."

He stood, dusting off his trousers. "Should be as good as new." He tested the dead bolt, which glided easily. "I rekeyed the front door to match it."

"Wow, Nathan. Thanks so much!"

He picked up a rag and wiped his brow. "Better be one helluva meal."

"Nothing like putting the pressure on."

He met her gaze. "No pressure. But I think I'd better go home and change first."

"That will give me time to stop by the store," Elizabeth said. "In the mood for anything special?"

His lips crept up in a grin. "Not sure you should ask that of a man who's half-dressed."

Her cheeks flamed. "I meant for dinner."

But he just stared at her in that ultra-sexy way that made her want to tackle him. Tackle him, and goodness knew what next. She was grateful they were having dinner with Claire. That would encourage Elizabeth to keep things under control. But what about when Claire went upstairs to do homework? A memory flashed through her mind of Nathan pinning her against the kitchen counter with hungry kisses, and her temperature spiked again. Elizabeth borrowed Nathan's rag to dab her own forehead.

"So, you're leaving the menu to my discretion?"

He studied her with amusement, then slipped back into his shirt.

"Whatever you and Claire would like will be great with me."

By the time Nathan got to Elizabeth's house, it was pouring. She let him in, dripping wet on the carpet. "You're soaked!"

"Maybe I didn't need to shower after all," he joked.

Claire appeared in the doorway, her eyes going wide. "Oh gosh," she told him, "I'll get a towel."

Nathan shrugged at Elizabeth. "Sky was clear as a bell until I started driving over."

"I know. The storm moved in fast!"

Thunder rumbled outside, accentuating that point.

Claire walked over and passed him a towel. "Thanks, hon," he told her. "Sure appreciate it."

He dried his hair and wiped off his clothing.

"Are you going to be okay in that?" Elizabeth asked. "I'd offer you a change, but…" She studied his physique and broad shoulders. "I don't have anything to fit you."

"I suspect not." He smiled at both her and Claire. "I'll be all right. I've endured tougher and lived to tell the tale."

"Have you?" Claire asked with interest. "Like what?"

"Nathan had some harrowing experiences out west."

"Really?" Claire asked with interest.

"I can tell you about it at dinner if you'd like," Nathan offered.

"That would be totally cool."

Elizabeth took Nathan's wet towel, eying his damp jeans and shirt with concern. "You sure you're all right?"

"Nothing a little wine won't fix." He handed a bottle in her direction.

She hadn't even seen him set it down on the table by the door when he'd hurried in. But that was Nathan. Always thinking of something. And it was always something nice. She was glad he'd invited himself over. That only saved her the trouble of having to ask him herself.

"Why don't we go in the kitchen and open it?"

A little while later, the three of them settled down to a comfortable dinner. Elizabeth made a roast chicken with stuffing and Southern green beans. Something homey but simple enough to prepare. Nathan sure seemed to appreciate his dinner. He even had seconds. "I can't remember chicken tasting this good." He stood to help clear the plates. "Thank you."

"Thanks for your help at my office today."

"And thanks for the stories," Claire said, carrying her dishes to the sink. "They were great." She turned to her mom, who was loading the dishwasher. "Did you know all that about him?"

Elizabeth smiled at her girl. "Some of it. The rest was news."

"Good thing you're a newspaper woman," Nathan said. "Otherwise, I might have bored you."

Claire and Elizabeth laughed.

"Mind if I skip dessert?" Claire asked her mom. "I've got a ton of algebra."

"That's one subject I can't help her with," Elizabeth confessed to Nathan.

"Let me know if you get stuck!" he called after the girl as she walked away.

Claire stopped and glanced over her shoulder with a pleased expression. "Thanks, Nathan."

"I can't believe it," Elizabeth said once Claire left. "You're good at math too?"

"Good enough," he told her. "Algebra's no problem anyway. I've had a recent refresher."

"What do you mean?"

"Melody had some trouble with it. I asked the school for an extra book so I could review and help her at home."

Elizabeth studied him with surprise.

"It's been a few years for me."

"No. I mean, I'm impressed that you'd do that, actually. You're a great uncle."

"Thanks."

"You'd make a great father too."

Elizabeth hung her head with a blush. "I mean…"

"I know what you mean," he said, "and I appreciate it."

"But you never…?"

"Married? No."

"Ever come close?"

Nathan appeared distant a moment, then met her gaze. When he did his eyes were full of emotion. "No one ever moved me in the right way." Her heart pounded. "The way that you do, Elizabeth."

"Nathan, I didn't mean to—"

He stepped toward her.

"It's all right to say what you feel. I've always believed too many folks don't."

Elizabeth felt caught up in his heat, as if she could barely breathe. When he stood this close, it was impossible to think straight. Hard to consider anything but being in his arms. "Maybe we should get some air."

"Now?" he asked, puzzled. "But it's raining cats and dogs."

"I was thinking we could have coffee on the porch. It's covered."

He glanced out the window and saw the rain had let up.

"I think coffee on the porch is a fine idea."

They sat and talked for a while in the darkness, the light pitter-patter of the rain keeping them company. The more Elizabeth learned about Nathan, the more she wanted to know. He was such an interesting man, and keen at offering insight. She valued his opinions on things, and he seemed equally engaged in hearing hers. She told him about her day and how the two interviews had gone. Janet had seemed in a particularly plucky mood, and she'd had a fresh flower tucked behind one ear. Nathan concealed a smile, then confessed that she and Bernie had been at odds the night before. They must have had one heck of a good time making up.

Elizabeth loved hearing the small-town lore and learning more about the fascinating people who lived here.

Everyone had a story to tell and was connected to each other in one way or another. The one thing Elizabeth found stunning was that nobody she'd talked to or had heard of appeared to be a native. All seemed to have arrived in Blayton from somewhere else.

"Is there no one in this town who was actually born here?"

Nathan rested his mug on his knee and stared at the house next door. "Mrs. Fenton was."

"Really?"

"Yeah. That was an old farmhouse. And all this here," he said, casting his gaze over the cemetery, "was original acreage."

"Her farm, you mean?"

"That's right."

Elizabeth heard a creaking sound and turned toward the house, startled to see one of the rockers suddenly tilting forward.

"The wind's picked up," Nathan explained.

That didn't excuse the slight shiver that ran down Elizabeth's spine. She took a sip of coffee to warm herself. "Right."

"You're not still spooked by that place?" he asked her.

"Not most days," she told him. "But Halloween's coming up."

"Ah, Halloween." He smiled in the shadows. "Ghosts, goblins, and such."

"You're not afraid of anything, are you?"

He studied her a beat. "I wasn't until recently."

"What are you scared of now?"

Instead of answering, he reached out and took her hand. He waited a long time before answering. When he did, his voice was raspy. "Don't go anywhere, all right?"

A lump welled in her throat because she knew what he really meant. He'd never been afraid of much, and the only thing that troubled him now was the prospect of losing her. She squeezed his hand, thinking she didn't want to lose him either. Not when it had taken her a lifetime to find him. The mood hung heavy with the moment, so neither one spoke. They just sat there together listening to the rain and watching the haze across the way.

Chapter Eleven

A few days later, Elizabeth and Claire were invited to dinner at Nathan's house. It was the least he could do, he said, after the hospitality they'd extended him. Elizabeth pulled into the drive of the small cottage hedging the orchard. It sat high on a hill and was ringed by mountains. Far on a distant ridge, she saw the first hint of snow, dusting tall pines in white powder.

"Nice, huh?" she said to Claire.

"Sure beats the heck out of our view."

It was twilight, the sky turning a purple-gray hue in the setting sun.

"Is it snowing up there?" Claire asked.

"Looks like."

"Cool. Wonder if we'll get any here?"

The temperature had dropped quite a bit, and both were dressed in jackets. Still, Elizabeth thought it was premature for snow where they were. "Probably not yet."

They strode toward the house together, Elizabeth carrying a bottle of wine.

Claire held a loaf of pumpkin bread that she'd made from scratch. "I won't mind it when it comes."

"Me either," Elizabeth said.

Nathan opened the front door before they got there, apparently having heard them drive up.

"Ladies… Well, what have we here?" he asked, accepting Claire's foil-wrapped package.

"She made it herself," Elizabeth informed him.

"Did you now?"

"Pumpkin bread. With raisins. Hope you like it."

He smiled at Claire with appreciation. "I'm sure I'll love it. Can't think of any kind of sweet bread I love more."

He let them in and took their jackets, thanking Elizabeth for her bottle of wine. "Something smells delicious."

"Brunswick stew. I thought it would be good with it getting colder out."

"Sounds great," Elizabeth said before Claire chimed in.

"We saw snow up there!"

"Snow?"

"In the higher elevations," Elizabeth explained.

"That's not unusual, I suppose. But we likely won't get any here yet."

Claire's face registered disappointment.

"Don't worry, young lady," Nathan told her. "Once the winter sets in, you might be singing a different tune."

"I doubt it."

"Claire loves the snow. We didn't get much in Richmond."

"Well, you'll get plenty here." Nathan led them to the cozy kitchen, where he'd set the table for three. It stood before a big bay window overlooking rows of apple trees.

"All that yours?" Claire wanted to know.

"The land is. But I've deeded the trees to Dan. He works them with the rest of his orchard, so I don't have to worry about it."

"Do you get anything in exchange?" Elizabeth wondered.

"All the apples a man could ask for." He laughed and opened a pantry door, exposing row upon row of preserved applesauce.

"Did you do all that yourself?" Elizabeth was impressed.

"I've had some long, lonely winters in Blayton." He met her eyes, and she flushed and turned away.

"You can take some home with you if you'd like. Mighty tasty heated up with pork chops."

"Or bacon and eggs?" Claire suggested.

"Those too."

"Can we, Mom?"

"Sounds like an offer we can't refuse." She glanced around the kitchen, spotting a large pot simmering on the stove and a tossed salad already made in a glass bowl on the counter. "Can we do anything to help?"

"Just eat like you appreciate it." He motioned for them to sit.

"Are you sure?" Elizabeth asked. "At least let me open the wine."

"Okay," he said with a wink. "If you insist."

They enjoyed a lovely meal as the sun went down and the landscape out the windows settled in shadows. Before long, it became dotted with flecks of white. "Guys, look!" Claire shouted happily.

Elizabeth eyed the scenery in awe. "Beautiful."

"Don't get too excited," Nathan said, standing to clear their plates. "Doubt it will last."

And, much to the women's disappointment, it didn't. By the time they'd helped clean up and stood saying good-bye, it had already stopped. Elizabeth had been having such a good time she didn't want the evening to end. The meal had been exquisite and the conversation among the three of them natural and easy. It was like one of those wooden puzzles with the different-shaped pegs and carved-out holes. Each of them fit in their own space, yet somehow they all worked together to complete a whole. Elizabeth was liking Nathan more and more, and she could tell Claire cared for him too. She never would have thought to make him pumpkin bread otherwise. She arrived at the idea all on her own.

"Thanks for the treat," he told Claire as they said good night on his front porch. "I can't wait to have some for breakfast."

Claire smiled happily, and Elizabeth met his eyes.

"Thank you," she said, "for everything." She had her jacket buttoned up against the chill and held two jars of applesauce.

"Good night, Elizabeth. I'm awfully glad the two of you could come."

"We'll have to do it again."

"When I don't have so much homework," Claire added.

The three of them laughed.

"Yes," Nathan said. "We'll work on that."

Elizabeth had already turned to leave when she spun back around.

"Halloween's this Friday," she began with a hopeful gaze.

His smile was sweet yet resigned. "Bernie and I are working. Busy night, even for this town. It will take the two of us to keep it running straight."

"Of course," she said, feeling disappointed nonetheless.

"We'll be making our rounds," he continued. "But that doesn't mean I can't check in on you during the night."

"We'll be home handing out candy," Elizabeth said.

They were nearly to the SUV when he called out to Claire. "Save some candy bars for me!"

He watched them drive away, a sudden melancholy in his heart. Nathan knew it made no sense to feel it, but he did just the same. Things seemed right when he was with the two of them. In some strange way, it was like they were always destined to be. One short month ago, he never could have imagined it. Now, it was hard to think of his life going forward without them. Elizabeth was extra special to him, but so was Claire. Nathan had never really known what it meant to be needed like a father. Though with Melody, he'd come close, he understood that he filled a different role for her. That of the loving uncle, which was just what Melody needed. Yet Claire didn't have any uncles in the picture, from what Elizabeth had shared. She didn't even have a surviving grandfather. Perhaps that was why she'd taken to Nathan the way she had. Even in becoming her mother's friend, he'd filled some sort of void. If things were to deepen between him and Elizabeth, he might close a still-larger gap. Nathan swallowed hard as he realized what he was thinking. And what he was thinking of was a future with Elizabeth and Claire.

"You could have kissed him good-bye, you know."

"*What?*"

They followed the winding country road over a one-lane bridge, Elizabeth's headlights leading the way.

"Come on, Mom. It's not like I don't have eyes."

"I don't know what you mean."

"I mean, you and the sheriff have been spending an awful lot of time together... *Hanging out.*"

Elizabeth felt her cheeks color. "That doesn't mean that—"

"How old do you think I am, anyway?"

"Fifteen."

"Sixteen, next month."

"Granted."

"That means I know."

Elizabeth glanced at her daughter. "Is this the voice of experience talking?" she asked, redirecting.

"I might have kissed a boy...*once*. No, wait, hang on a minute. Make that two times."

"Claire Victoria!" Elizabeth exclaimed "Perry?"

"Oh, Mom," she said in a dreamy way. "Do you think it's possible to fall in love at my age?"

Elizabeth thought hard about this. "I think people fall in love at all kinds of ages. From the young to the very old."

"How about people your age?"

Elizabeth pursed her lips a beat before answering. "I won't lie to you and say I don't care for Nathan."

"That's good."

Claire settled back in her seat and offered nothing more.

Elizabeth was too stunned to say much herself. There she was, unable to admit her true feelings to herself. And her fifteen-year-old daughter had nailed them.

They drove the rest of their way home in silence, but there was a happy new camaraderie between them. Mother and daughter, both sharing their confidences. Each having an inkling of how the other one felt.

Perry angled his body toward Claire and planted his palm against her locker. It was only nine in the morning, but already it couldn't have been a better day. She'd never known a cuter boy. She'd never kissed one either. Fact was, she'd never kissed anybody before at all. And when Perry had done it, he'd rocked her world.

"So," he told her, "I was thinking I might stop by later. You know, to hear the rest of that song you're writing for me?"

"You're such an egomaniac."

"I thought you liked that about me. The idea that I have confidence."

She repressed a grin but knew there were stars in her eyes. "Yeah, I do."

"And I," he said, leaning closer, "like that about you."

"Two minutes!" Mrs. Carole said, striding past them. She clutched her teacher planner to her chest and walked in brisk steps.

"Aye, aye!" Perry said, saluting her as she strode away.

Claire giggled.

"How is it that all the teachers here like you?"

"Most of the teachers," he confessed, "are female."

"What a player." She gave an exaggerated sigh. "Don't tell me you're into cougar territory?"

"Not a chance."

Joy and her friends passed by, and he waved to them.

"Only one girl at Blayton's caught my eye."

"So," she said in a flirty way. "I was wondering about Friday...?"

"That's Halloween," he said, growing serious.

"I was thinking maybe you could come over? Help me give out candy? I know it sounds lame, but—"

Perry dropped his hand. "I'm sorry, Claire. You don't know how sorry I am. But we're into full harvest time at the orchard, and I promised my uncle—"

"I understand."

"If there was a way—"

"No, really."

She met his eyes but still suspected her gaze was melancholy.

"Tell you what," he said, nudging her chin. "What if I drop by Saturday morning? Take you out for the day?"

Claire's mood brightened. "Where?"

"Anywhere in the world you'd like to go."

"That leaves things wide open."

"Just think about it," he said as the first-period bell rang.

Janet stared at Bernie agape when he walked in the Dollar Store. "What are you doing here?"

"Visiting."

"You never visit when I'm working."

"I know."

He began surveying the aisles as if he was searching for something, but Janet knew differently.

"Bernie, what's going on?"

"I made a decision this morning," he said, "and I wanted you to know about it."

"Huh?"

"I think we should have kids."

Janet turned fifty shades of pale. "Were you out drinking last night?"

"No! I had the night beat. You know that."

She glanced around the store. Only a few patrons were there, and they were way in the back, sifting through the sales bin. Two for a dollar. That was a deal.

"Then what's this all about?"

Bernie walked right up to her and set his hands on the counter. "I'm done messing around." She blinked but he kept going. "I mean it. I know I haven't always been the best husband. I mean, I've supported you when I could—"

She reached out and touched his arm. "Did you take your morning supplements?"

"Yeah, yeah." He shook his head. "Are you even listening to me?"

"I'm listening." She looked at him askance. "But forgive me for saying you're coming off a little weird."

This was a new one, Bernie thought but didn't say. Instead, his voice rose with emotion. "Baby, I realize what I've been doing wrong."

She fingered the crystal hanging on a hemp chain around her neck. "Huh?"

"It's true," he said with earnest eyes. "I haven't valued you the way I should. But I understand it all now. I *get* you."

Her beautiful eyes widened.

"You're a little bit quirky, a little bit *out there*—"

"Hey!"

"But, darling, there's nobody on this earth I'd rather be with. Nobody I know who would make a finer mom. That's why I threw out my last cigarette last night."

"You didn't."

"I did," he proclaimed.

"Oh Bernie!" She leaned across the counter to pull him close. After a pause, she whispered in his ear, "You're not messing with me, are you?"

"Never."

She studied him forever, her lips scrunched up in thought. Then, to Bernie's surprise, she removed her glasses and shared a sultry gaze.

"Then meet me at home at one." Her voice was a low purr. "Darleen's coming in, and I've got a lunch break."

Martha eyed Lex above the rim of her book with a suspicious air. He stood there with a box of chocolate caramels. Her favorites.

"Brought you a little surprise to have with your afternoon coffee."

"Uh-oh. What did you do?" She set down her book and narrowed her gaze. "Better to tell me now than have me hanging in suspense till I get home." The way he had when he blew up their dryer after rewiring the laundry room himself. Martha hadn't even realized appliances could spit out clothes! Apparently they did when they were angry enough. "You haven't been messing with that satellite dish on the roof again?"

"Honey," he said with a big, bold grin. "It's fixed!"

"What's fixed?"

"The town! Internet, broadband, Wi-Fi... Everything! Go on, check!"

She picked up her cell and scanned it for bars, but her face hung in disappointment.

"Okay," he admitted. "So the cell towers still need work. But try your computer! Go ahead!"

She surveyed him doubtfully but then swiveled her chair toward her desktop PC, which was situated to the side. She hit a couple of buttons and clicked the mouse.

"Well...?" he asked with hopeful anticipation.

The computer hummed, booting up, then whirred into action, message alerts sounding. She stared at the screen, her mouth fixed in a scowl. But her pout was pretend.

"Now you've done it."

"Whaaat, sugar? What's wrong?"

"I've got over three hundred emails to answer." She turned to him, her expression brightening. "Oh Lex, it's true! The station's back in business!"

"Everything's back in business. That's what I've been trying to tell you. I mean, I know it's been a long haul, and folks were getting frustrated—"

She leapt to her feet and wrapped him in a hug. "I never doubted you for a minute!"

Joy walked in the door carrying her backpack. She generally caught the bus here after school to see her mom before stopping by the library to do homework. Now her eyes were on her parents, standing in an enraptured embrace. She noted the chocolates on the desk.

"What's going on?" She was obviously puzzled. "It's not your anniversary?"

Martha released Lex and smoothed out her sweater. "Your daddy fixed the Internet!"

"Me and my friends," he corrected. But he wore a proud mug.

"Seriously?" Joy's eyes lit up as she pumped the air with her fist. "*Ye-es!*"

Chapter Twelve

By Halloween, everyone in Blayton was in great spirits. Claire had been able to communicate with her old friends and now felt more at peace about her sudden good-bye. She told Elizabeth maybe it was good they'd been out of touch for a while. Gave her time to settle in and really feel a part of this new town so when she wrote to them she had something positive to say. Elizabeth had even gotten through to Jerry. She'd emailed him a draft of her first edition, and he'd loved every word.

The evening temperatures had dropped into the thirties, and last night they got their first hard frost. Claire walked across the lawn to her bus stop by the road, and brittle grass crunched beneath her.

"Have a great day!" Elizabeth said from the front porch. She was bundled in her work clothes and a throw blanket to ward off the cold. In one hand, she held a coffee mug. With the other, she motioned to the large orange pumpkin that perched on the porch step. "You going to carve that when you get home?"

"You bet!" Claire called as the bus pulled up.

When Elizabeth went back inside, the house phone was ringing. She picked it up and heard a familiar masculine voice. "I wanted to be the first… Well, maybe among the first. Claire may have said it already…to wish you a happy Halloween!"

Elizabeth laughed merrily. "Good morning, Nathan. And happy Halloween to you!"

"You gals all ready?"

Her gaze fell to the stocked bowl of candy by the front door. "Well, we've got plenty of treats, that's for sure."

"Just as long as there are no tricks tonight, we'll be in business."

"I guess that's what you're helping to ensure."

"Bernie and I will be patrolling, but I don't expect much trouble this go-round."

"Have you had any in the past?"

There was a long pause on the line.

"Nothing much to speak of," he finally said. "Mostly kids playing pranks."

"Doesn't sound like anything you and Bernie can't handle."

"I think our having a presence is disincentive enough."

Elizabeth breathed easily knowing Blayton was a safer place just because Nathan was a part of it. He was a dynamite man and an excellent sheriff. "Any idea what time you'll be stopping by?"

"It will probably be around nine o'clock. Is that too late?"

"No," she said with a contented heart. For she always felt at peace when he was in the picture. "It's perfect."

Nathan hung up the phone feeling disconcerted. He hadn't precisely lied to Elizabeth, but he hadn't exactly told her the truth either. The fact was, there had been a bit of trouble in Blayton a few years back: a mysterious disappearance that nobody could explain. An entire family had gone missing sometime late on Halloween night, and he and Bernie had never found the reason behind it. From all appearances, it seemed like they'd just suddenly packed up and gone. There were no signs of a struggle and no indications of foul play. The husband and wife had both been teachers at the high school. It was just the two of them and their small baby, a toddler, really, who went for daycare with some of the other children in town at Mrs.

Robeson's. She ran an at-home service that seemed to bring her great joy. She was a kindly older woman, and she and her elderly husband, the realtor, Bob, had never had kids of their own.

The family mostly kept to themselves and didn't connect too strongly to anyone else in town, not even any of the school personnel he and Bernie questioned later. The only person the wife seemed to have taken into her confidence was Mrs. Robeson. When they arrived here, their child was gravely ill, though none of the town's folk knew it. He had a serious blood condition, something related to childhood leukemia. The parents were devastated and had pretty much given up on putting him through the grueling treatments. The doctors said they were futile at that point anyway, and they caused the child such misery he cried with a colicky air throughout the night. The family had come to Blayton to get away from the doctors and the limelight of a larger town and find a way to bring their family peace. The odd thing was, the day before they'd gone away, the mother told Mrs. Robeson the baby had spontaneously been getting better. Mrs. Robeson could attest to that fact too. After what seemed an eternity of pallor, there was finally color in his cheeks and his appetite was improving. He'd even said his first words and taken a few tentative toddler steps. As far as Mrs. Robeson could see, he was well on his way to becoming a normal child. But the next thing she knew, the Parker family was gone.

Nathan sank heavily in his chair and gazed out the window, where the morning sun was just shedding light on the neighboring shops. *Poof!* Gone. Just like that. Just like Belle and Melody… And the Carletons last spring. Emma Gray and her mom, the season before. Nathan shook his head to clear it, thinking he was connecting dots where there was no logical connection. As old-fashioned as it seemed, in many ways Blayton was a modern town. And in modern towns, people came and went all the time. Nothing so unusual about that. Perry's Uncle Dan had arrived here four years ago. His nephew had joined him the following summer. And Elizabeth and Claire had gotten here just last month. There really wasn't anything more constant in life than change. And Blayton wasn't any exception. The only thing that made it exceptional now was the fact that the Jennings had moved in. Those were two people Nathan didn't want leaving any time soon. Not if that meant they'd be leaving here without him. He wasn't quite sure he could take that. Not with what his heart was starting to feel.

Perry and Claire took their seats at their new lunch spot. It had been getting too cold to eat outdoors, so they'd moved inside. Joy and Lilly had surprised them by offering to share their table. While Claire never might have imagined it a few weeks ago, she and the other girls were becoming friends. She glanced across the crowded cafeteria and saw Penelope eating by herself. "I hate it that she sits there alone."

"I know," Joy agreed. "But she did it to herself."

"Said she wouldn't stay here if you two barged in," Lilly blurted out.

Joy elbowed her.

"Ouch!" She glanced at Perry and Claire. "Sorry."

"Still," Claire said. "It rots to be having such a great day when someone else looks so miserable."

"What's so great about it?" Perry asked. "Other than it's Halloween, and you know…" He wiggled his eyebrows, and the other girls laughed. "We all get to eat mega candy tonight."

"We're supposed to be handing it out," Lilly interjected. "Not eating it ourselves."

"I thought we were supposed to be dividing it?" Perry glanced around with mock innocence. "You know, one for you, you cute little goblin, and a great big handful for me?"

Claire slapped him with a laugh. "Shut up. You're not going to be stealing any kid's candy."

"I didn't say stealing, I said—"

She met his eyes with a challenge. "Don't you even want to hear why I'm having such a great day?"

"Well, yeah, sure. Other than the part about you're already sitting here with me."

He preened a bit, strumming his chest with his fingers.

"He's been impossible since I said I'd go out with him," Claire told the other girls.

They shook their heads, but neither one appeared as if she'd mind going out with Perry herself.

"Anyway," Claire continued, "here's my big news." When she shared it, she practically squealed. "I got a B+ on my algebra exam!"

"Way...to...go!" Perry high-fived her, and the other two did as well.

Claire was so pleased with herself she felt she was bursting. It was the best grade she'd gotten in math all year. Didn't hurt that Nathan had been helping her with the homework. He had a simple way of explaining things that made them less complicated. Plus, he didn't yell at her for asking questions, the way her uptight teacher Mrs. Peabody did.

She surprised the rest of the table by getting to her feet.

"Where are you going?" asked Joy.

"I just had an idea about Penelope," Claire said, glancing her way.

She strode across the cafeteria and plopped down across from Penelope at her table. Rather than appearing welcoming, the other girl shot her an acrimonious look.

"You don't have to eat here all alone, you know."

"I'm my own best company," Penelope replied with a smirk.

Though Claire doubted that, she didn't say so. She opted to take a different tact. "Rough test today, huh?"

"It sucked." Penelope's expression was gloomy. "Mrs. Peabody sucks. She's a horrible teacher."

"She's not the most patient one at Blayton, that's for sure."

"Probably means she's working on it."

"What makes you say that?"

"My mom says that everyone in life is working on something."

Claire considered this a moment, secretly wondering what Penelope was working on. She hoped it wasn't replacing Melody as prime school bully. "Well, maybe she is," she finally answered.

Penelope stopped chewing a moment to stare at her. "Are you here for something?"

"I, uh… Yeah. Actually, I am."

Penelope waited.

Claire had seen the way Penelope quickly folded over her paper after peeking at her grade. Mrs. Peabody had a really mean habit of handing back test grades in order—highest first. It was obvious to all Penelope had gotten the lowest mark in the class.

"I was thinking that maybe I could help you with algebra?"

"Help me? But aren't you the one Mrs. Peabody's always yelling at?"

"I'm learning to ignore her."

Penelope scrutinized her a moment. She'd obviously noticed that Claire's paper had been handed out early on. "How did *that* help you get a better grade?"

"It wasn't Mrs. Peabody that helped. It was Nathan."

"The sheriff?"

"Yeah."

"But how...?" Her eyes registered understanding. "I get it. He's dating your mom."

"Something like that." Claire pursed her lips, thinking how fast news traveled in a small town. "Anyhow, the point is, he's helped me understand it a lot better, so I was thinking...maybe I could help you?"

Penelope eyed her suspiciously. "Why?"

"Because I think you're kind of like Melody."

Her face reddened. "Melody's gone."

"Yeah, she is. She also wasn't as mean as she wanted everybody to think." Claire studied her. "Neither are you."

Penelope glanced at the table where Perry and the other two girls were eating and pretending not to watch. "Is this some kind of weird Halloween joke?"

"Nope."

"Are you like...going out for sainthood or something?"

Claire sighed with exasperation. "Penelope, why don't you just say yes?"

"Maybe I like things the way they are." But Claire could tell that she didn't.

"You like failing math class? That's crazy, because I didn't."

"You were failing?"

"Think about it. Whose paper always got handed out last?"

Penelope studied her a beat, but Claire could tell her mood was softening. "I don't know. I think maybe it's too late."

"Too late for what?"

"I don't understand any of the questions I got wrong. I mean, I don't even know *why* I got them wrong. They still look right to me."

Claire eyed her with sympathy. "I've got some time after school."

"I've got to watch my little sister."

"How about if I meet you both at the library?"

"I don't get it. Why would you do that for me?"

Claire answered her truthfully. "I don't know. It's just something I think I should do."

"No tricks?"

"No tricks." She paused a moment, then whispered, "But you can bring some treats if you want."

"We're not supposed to eat in the library," Penelope whispered back.

Claire lowered her voice further with a giggle. "I won't tell if you won't."

To her utter amazement, Penelope smiled. And it wasn't a little one either. It was one of those great big, blooming, knock-me-over-with-a-feather grins.

"Okay, Claire," Penelope said with a nod. "You've got yourself a deal."

Later that afternoon, Elizabeth closed up her newspaper office, feeling contented. She'd gotten a call from Claire saying she was meeting a friend at the library so had stayed an extra hour to tidy up. She'd had interview notes and sample photographs strewn everywhere and piles of rough drafts sitting around. Elizabeth viewed the ancient typewriter she'd displayed in the front window with satisfaction. Even an old-school writer would have approved of the effort she'd turned out. The newspaper had hit the Internet, and she'd been flooded by emails and calls from appreciative residents. It was so nice she'd gotten the weekly paper running again. People especially favored the *Swap, Bake, or Barter* section, where residents could trade one set of skills or goods for another without having to lay out precious cash. Elizabeth was proud of the fact that this had been her idea. Somehow it seemed to fit a town like Blayton to a tee. Jerry found it very "down-home" and hoped his reporters might mimic the concept in other small towns.

Not bad for a first month's work, Elizabeth mused, locking up. The key in her hand reminded her of another accomplishment. She'd made friends with a handsome, single man. Okay, she'd admit it. More than friends. Elizabeth found herself falling desperately, head-over-heels in love with Nathan. How could she not? He was everything a woman like her could hope for. Not only that, he was extra kind to her daughter. Elizabeth could tell he wasn't putting it on. Nathan's interest in Claire was authentic. Elizabeth didn't know how they'd been so lucky to have him come into their lives when he did. But his timing couldn't have been more perfect. Elizabeth had spent a lifetime wondering if the kind of love she'd read about in books and had seen in movies truly existed. Now that she found herself falling for Nathan, she realized it actually did. Hers wasn't some schoolgirl crush or nonsensical longing. Rather, it was a deep-seated feeling that Nathan was right for her. Right for them. She respected Nathan and admired him greatly. And when he took her in his arms, she melted—like snow beneath a warming sun. *You couldn't do better than that,* Elizabeth thought as dusk closed in. *I couldn't do better than that.*

Chapter Thirteen

A full moon rose in the night sky, and brisk winds whistled through the trees. They were bare now, having shed all their leaves. Their limbs stretched like craggy fingers up toward the clouds, shrouding the moon from time to time. Claire carried her carved jack-o'-lantern to the front porch and lit the candle she'd positioned inside it. It was only seven o'clock but pitch black with occasional moonlight casting a haunting glow. The little kids would have a blast tonight. And she and her mom were ready. They had enough candy to fortify a horde of trick-or-treaters. Hey, if enough kids didn't come around, Claire had agreed in advance to share her spoils with Perry.

Despite all his ribbing at lunchtime today, Perry wouldn't really be handing out goodies. Instead, he'd be helping his uncle prepare produce shipping boxes. Claire liked that about Perry. The fact that he was responsible. Sure he was a loudmouth and a show-off sometimes, but in truth he was a down-to-earth guy who worked hard to do the right thing. He'd told her about how special his uncle was. After Perry's parents' and little brother's tragic deaths, Dan had taken him in. No questions, no doubts. They were family, and Perry belonged with Dan. It was hard for Perry not to think about the hurricane or all he'd tried to do to save his little brother. But sometimes nature took the upper hand, and for whatever reason there was, Perry had been left on his own after the storm surge had subsided. Claire felt awful for Perry having gone through that, but knew it was a blessing his kind Uncle Dan had taken him in. He'd told her he was grateful too. His uncle was very important to him. There was nobody Perry loved more. Up until now, that was.

"I guess we're ready," Elizabeth said, appearing on the porch. "I wonder if we'll get many kids tonight."

"At least a few," Claire answered. "I mean, who can resist trick-or-treating across from a graveyard?"

"Or beside a haunted house?"

"Exactly."

A burst of air blew through, extinguishing the jack-o'-lantern's candle.

"*Mo-om?*" Claire said as the rocker at the house next door began to creak.

"It's all right," Elizabeth said, patting her back. "Only the wind."

"More like Phantom!" Claire pointed at the cat, who'd just sprung out of a rocker on Mrs. Fenton's porch and jumped up on another.

Elizabeth laughed. "Why don't you call him over?"

"I'll go and get him."

Phantom purred loudly at her approach. But the moment Claire set her foot on the stoop's lower step, she regretted her decision. A chill raced down her spine so icy that gooseflesh rose on her arms. "Come here, you stupid cat," she said, reaching for him. Claire pulled him out of the chair and carted him back to her brightly lit house that looked almost like heaven from here.

Claire knew she was being lame, getting spooked just because it was Halloween. They couldn't help that they lived beside a creepy old house any more than they could that they lived across the street from a graveyard. Cemetery. Whatever. She actually thought the two words were synonyms but wasn't about to argue with her mom, the newspaper editor. Elizabeth had gone back indoors to get the bowl of candy they'd prepared. There was a low table by one of the chairs on the front porch that made the perfect candy-bowl holder. They planned to sit on the porch and visit while waiting on the trick-or-treaters. Later, when Nathan stopped by, maybe the three of them would watch a scary movie. But that was only if he could stay. Claire wasn't sure she wanted to watch anything too frightening with just her and her mom around. Not that she was superstitious or anything, or believed in ghosts.

"Think we'll get anybody?" she asked when she returned with Phantom.

Elizabeth glanced toward the walk and a minivan that was parked at the end of their drive. "Here come some now." Three little girls, all dressed like fairy princesses, paraded toward the porch, their dad walking protectively behind them.

Claire set Phantom down in a rattan chair and stroked him as he curled into a ball.

"Aren't you cute!" Elizabeth said as they held out their plastic pumpkins.

"Aren't you going to say something first?" Claire prodded, lifting the candy bowl.

"Trick or treat!" the three little ones squealed.

Claire had to admit they were pretty adorable. All accepted their treats with polite thanks as their dad nodded from behind. This was actually kind of fun, Claire decided. Being on the grown-up side of things. The only thing that would make it better would be having Perry here. But she would see him tomorrow. The two of them had already made plans.

"Think I'm going to go on in the house to make coffee," Elizabeth said after several more groups had come and gone. It seemed parents in Blayton were eager to help their kids comb the town for treats, even if that meant driving out into the countryside. "Want anything?"

"I'm fine," Claire said, preparing to man the fort. She rested the candy bowl on her knees and waited. A little ways down the road, she spied a new group of kids arriving on bicycles. These seemed a little older and didn't have any parents with them. Elizabeth followed her gaze to the boys.

"Want me to wait until after these guys are gone?"

"No big deal," Claire said. "I'll handle it."

Nathan steered his cruiser down the narrow gravel lane. The former Parker place was worth checking on. He'd caught three middle schoolers there last year. They'd snuck in with sleeping bags and dared each other to last the night. A few of them even planned to record their ghost hunting on handhelds. Nathan had scared them badly when he'd shot the beam of his flashlight through the front window. Who knew what they thought he was. A ghost, probably, Nathan thought with a chuckle.

He pulled into the drive, his headlights illuminating the sturdy Cape Cod. It had been built to withstand the mountain winds and was set in a scenic valley. Yet nobody had wanted to rent the house since the Parkers and their toddler disappeared from there two years ago tonight. While it appeared sunny and inviting by daylight, the streaming moonlight gave its dark windows a ghostly glow. Things seemed pretty peaceful from here, but he'd get out of his car and take a closer look on foot just to make sure.

As the kids drew near the porch, Claire saw they were older than she originally suspected. Probably seventh or eighth graders. At that age where they were too old to trick-or-treat but wanted the candy just the same. All were dressed in army camouflage pants with dark T-shirts, their faces smudged in black. Rather than carrying kiddy-like plastic pumpkins, they clutched large pillowcases already sagging with their haul. "Hey!" one of them said. "It's the ghost cat!"

Phantom raised his head from the chair nearby to stare at him.

"He's not a ghost cat," Claire said mildly. She positioned the bowl in front her and raised her eyebrows.

But instead of saying the expected phrase, the kids remained fixated on Phantom.

"He's creepy," the second one said. "See how the light from the jack-o'-lantern catches in his eyes?"

Claire saw Phantom's eyes glow orangey gold in the candlelight flickers but knew that was a natural phenomenon.

"Isn't that the cat that used to belong to Mrs. Fenton?"

"The one who *ate her*?" another one asked.

"Do you guys want any candy or what?"

Phantom rose to stretch his legs and arched his back high. "Here, kitty, kitty!" one boy called, while another one surprised them all by suddenly shouting, "Boo!"

His friends nearly jumped out of their skins, and he roared with laughter.

Phantom leapt from the chair and darted off the porch.

"Now look what you've done," Claire scolded. "Phantom!" she called after him as he ran for the road. "No!"

A car was approaching, driving much too fast for Halloween night. It sped toward the cat, and Claire's heart pounded. "Geez!" She set down the bowl and chased after him. "Phantom, move!"

A dark ball of fur sped out of the way of the car just in time. The car's horn blared as the driver zoomed away.

"Slow down!" Claire yelled after him, though she knew it was futile.

Claire scanned the surrounding area, searching for Phantom. *There he is! Right across the road.* The cat tore through a row of tombstones and headed up the hill, moving fast. "Phantom!" Claire called, chasing after him. "Wait!"

Nathan walked around the last corner of the house, shining the beam of his flashlight on the windows. Everything checked out here tonight. No mischief from the Bailey boys, three brothers all born within three years. *Irish triplets*, Martha said that was called. The poor Bailey parents had their hands full with that lot. The luck of the Irish certainly wasn't with them there. Those kids were into everything and almost always in detention at school. But Nathan knew they weren't bad to the core. They just had some kinks to work out, and they would someday. Each of them had potential. And all exhibited that more when they were apart rather than huddled together in some lamebrain scheme.

Nathan returned to his cruiser, thinking how lucky Elizabeth was to have Claire. She was a great kid on her own and didn't need a lot of coaxing. He checked the time on the dash and saw it was close to nine. He'd drop by for a visit now to see how they were doing. There clearly wasn't any action going on here.

As he backed his car out of the drive, Nathan glanced up at the night sky. A big, round moon danced in and out of dark clouds, sending bright light streaming earthward in sudden waves. One of them caught in his rearview mirror, causing it to shimmer. Nathan found himself thinking of the Parkers, then of Melody Anne and Belle, and all the other folks that had come and gone from this town. His eyes slowly returned to the mirror as he observed those familiar hazel eyes, the contours of that face... Something gripped him from the inside out, and then with a bolt of understanding, Nathan *knew.*

He jammed his foot on the brake and put the car in Park, his whole reality reeling. His motions seemed surreal as he reached for his radio and called for his deputy.

"All clear here," Bernie said. His voice crackled through the airwaves. "How are things there?"

Nathan told himself to stay calm and keep his breathing measured. "Bernie," he said, "I need you to promise me something."

"What's the matter, Chief? What's going on?"

"Just say you'll promise, all right?"

"You need back... I'm... You know that." His voice was fading in and out, coming through in incomplete words. "... location?"

Nathan's tone was steady, commanding. "Have I ever asked anything of you before? Anything personal?"

Their connection rippled and snapped with electric current before Bernie finally answered.

"No."

"Then here's what I need you to do..."

Bernie stared out his squad car window in disbelief. He could see Elizabeth's newspaper office straight ahead of him, with the Dollar Store and a few other shops aligned to the left. The business district was nearly silent, with all shops closed up tight and only a few lonely street lamps shedding their light.

"What do you mean, *if I don't see you again for a while?*" Bernie clutched the radio, his temples pounding. "Where are you going?"

"I need you to give me a ten-four on that, buddy."

But he couldn't! Just couldn't promise to take over and run things for Nathan! Bernie barely got by as a deputy. *I haven't got what it takes to be sheriff.* "Chief, I can't... Don't know how—"

"Martha will help you. Everyone in Blayton will."

"You can't do this! Just up and—"

"Signing off now."

"Nathan!"

"Give me a *Roger*."

Bernie hung his head in disbelief, though somehow he suspected Nathan was giving him no choice. "I read you," he said, his voice cracking.

"Copy back. Over and..."

But the line sizzled and popped, cutting off his final word.

When Elizabeth returned to the porch, she found Claire gone and three boys raiding the candy bowl. "Hey! Where's—?"

"Run!" They shoved fistfuls of treats into pillowcases and took off on their bikes, scattering in all directions.

Elizabeth frantically scanned the yard, searching for Claire. There! Across the street! She saw her pacing back and forth between the headstones on the hill. Elizabeth reached into the house and snagged her jacket from the hook by the door. Then, she was off, walking briskly toward her daughter in the cemetery.

Claire called softly to Phantom as he slunk along ahead of her, winding his way around tombstones. "Here, kitty, kitty! Here, boy!" The clouds parted, exposing a big, yellow moon. It lit up the graveyard like a spotlight, casting long shadows behind grave markers that stood like silent towers in the night. Claire shivered in the brisk air but kept going. She was nearly to her cat, who had paused before a large headstone and now turned to stare at her, his head held high. Claire reached forward and snatched him off the ground, drawing him to her chest. "Phantom! You crazy cat!" She held him tighter, her gaze skimming the marker in front of her. Then suddenly Claire's blood ran cold.

"What on earth are you doing…?" Elizabeth began. Her mom must have crossed the street and come up behind her, but Claire hadn't heard her at all. Instead, her eyes were fixed on the tombstone straight ahead and the name written upon it: *Melody Anne Richards.*

Claire's heart pounded, and her throat felt like it was swelling shut.

"Did you come up here chasing that…?" Elizabeth caught her breath with a gasp. "What on earth?"

Claire's gaze traveled to the headstone beside Melody's and found it belonged to *Belle.* She swallowed hard.

"This is crazy," Elizabeth said. "Somebody must be playing a joke."

"Elizabeth!" It was Nathan's voice. "Claire!"

They turned to find him heading up the hill with his flashlight. His cruiser was parked at their house across the street. Phantom squirmed in Claire's arms, and she set him down as Nathan came near.

"Thank God," Elizabeth breathed. He rushed to her, and she leapt into his arms. "Something horrible is going on."

Nathan pulled back from her hug to glance at Claire. "Are you all right?"

But what could she say? It was like she couldn't find the words. Even if she could, they wouldn't come out. So Claire just pointed.

Nathan followed her gaze, then pulled them to him, hugging one in each arm. "I want you to listen to me, both of you. Everything's going to be okay." He looked at them with reassurance "*We're* going to be okay."

"But...how?" Elizabeth's chin trembled. "How is that possible?"

Nathan met her eyes and said softly, "I think you know."

"What?"

"Elizabeth. Claire," he said, "I want you to think back. Think hard. Was there ever a time... A time when you had a close call? A time when you thought you'd...?"

She broke his embrace, stepping away.

"That's ridiculous," Elizabeth said. "Do you hear what you're saying?"

Claire strode toward her mom. "I think we need to listen to him."

Elizabeth gaped at her daughter in disbelief.

Claire spoke softly now. "What about that time in the—?"

"No!" Elizabeth shouted. Tears streamed down her cheeks.

Nathan spoke softly from behind them. "I need to tell you something. Something I didn't even know until just a few moments ago."

Twigs snapped in the distance, and they stared higher up the hill to the very last row of graves. There were two of them at the top, the new ones Elizabeth had seen going in the day they moved here.

"It's Phantom!" Claire cried. The cat wound his way around the headstones, casting them a backward glance over his shoulder.

Nathan met Elizabeth's eyes. "Remember when I told you about my camping trip? That blizzard where I was avalanched in for ten days?"

Elizabeth stared at him, unable to speak.

"You asked me how I survived it…"

Somewhere in the distance, a hoot owl called.

"Elizabeth," he said. "I didn't."

Ice tore through her veins, and she felt faint.

"Just wha…what are you saying?"

"I need you and Claire to think back. Try to remember."

Claire's voice was a hoarse whisper. "The truck."

Nathan glanced at Elizabeth.

"It can't be. It's not possible."

"Mom was driving me home from my guitar lessons," Claire told Nathan. "It was raining hard. There was a truck on the highway. Guy must have been drunk or fallen asleep."

"He crossed over the line," Elizabeth said in a monotone.

"He was coming straight at us," Claire continued.

"But no!" Elizabeth cried with panicked certainty. "I swerved! We swerved to avoid it."

Nathan studied her with sympathy, his heart breaking for her. "There wasn't time."

Elizabeth's face twisted with anguish. *"No."*

"Yes, Elizabeth," he whispered gently. "I'm afraid so."

Claire's mouth fell open, and Nathan motioned the girl to him. He pulled her into a hug and her mother too. "This can't be right," Elizabeth said, as tears leaked from her eyes. "What about my job? What about the paper?"

Nathan spoke under his breath, his words carrying the weight of truth. "There is no paper. At least, not one beyond Blayton. You needed a reason to come here. A reason you could believe in."

"But if I didn't come here for work, then…"

Her cloudy expression cleared, and her face registered understanding. "I came here for you, didn't I? We…" She glanced at Claire. "We were meant to find you."

There was acknowledgement in his eyes. "Everyone comes to Blayton for a reason. There are things we need to settle. Once we settle those scores, it's time to move on."

"What about my old friends?" Claire asked him. "The ones back in Richmond? I talked to them yesterday."

"The truth, hon? I don't think they got your posts. Just like Jerry never heard from your mom. These were things you felt you needed to do. But people in Blayton have no real contact with the outside world. I'm convinced of that now. The most serious business we're meant to take care of is what gets done here."

"But I don't want to leave," Elizabeth said. She cast a longing gaze across the way at their little house that was already fading in the fog. Phantom had scampered back across the road and settled in on Mrs. Fenton's front porch, where he curled up in a rocker. She glanced at Claire, then once again met Nathan's eyes. "We were just starting to feel at home."

"We can make a new home together."

Claire's face brightened. "You're coming with us?"

"I'm taking you."

Elizabeth's heart brimmed with happiness. She and Claire would always feel safe with Nathan along. He loved them both, and they loved him. She knew this with utter certainty, although none of them had spoken the words. "Where are we going?"

Nathan motioned with his chin to the mountain's highest ridge. "Over there."

He took Elizabeth by the hand and held Claire's hand on the other side.

"How long have you known?" Elizabeth asked him.

"It only hit me this evening. Once you start to understand, it all becomes clear."

"But Belle…? How did she…?"

"I suspect some folks get longer to adjust than others. Must depend on what you've got left to do."

"And who you're leaving behind?" Elizabeth asked.

"Yes."

"Claire!"

Claire turned with joy to see Perry and Dan standing at the base of the graveyard. "Perry! Up here!"

He and his uncle headed their way as tears streamed down Claire's cheeks.

"Wait for us!" Dan called. "We're coming with you!"

They hustled up the hill, and Perry took Claire's hand. "I didn't want to go without you."

"Not a chance of that."

Elizabeth stretched out her free hand. "Dan, come on." He walked over and linked his hand with hers.

"I thought I was pretty lucky to survive that landmine," he told Nathan with a laugh.

Nathan set his chin with understanding. "I'm sure Belle's waiting to hear all about it."

The wind whistled through the trees as they all stood there together, a human chain linked together by more than just their hands. Clouds rolled across the sky, shrouding the moon, and the fog closed in.

"What do we do now?" Elizabeth asked.

Nathan firmly held Claire's hand and squeezed hers. "Just close your eyes."

Epilogue

A few weeks later, a new SUV rolled into town. Young dad, Alex Marshall, couldn't believe his rotten luck. The house had seemed fine in the online listing, but here it was situated across the street from a graveyard.

"Cool," eight-year-old Winston said. "Do you think there are ghosts?"

At least his boy wasn't afraid. Good thing too, given that creepy old Victorian next door.

Alex thumped on his GPS, noting the screen had gone black. "Well, we certainly can't be in the middle of nowhere!" he told his kid with a laugh.

"Dad, look!" Winston pointed to a big tabby cat that was scampering up the steps to their new home. "Do you think it belongs to anybody?"

Alex popped open his driver's door. "Something tells me we're going to find out."

He studied the scenery before him, thinking it wasn't all bad. They'd had a light dusting of snow yesterday evening, and now everything, including the tops of the tombstones, were dusted in powdery white. *But what's that?* Alex rubbed his chin, feeling sorry for those poor souls who had to dig three new graves this close to winter. Ground must be as hard as ice.

A car driving by on the country road pulled off to the side, and an attractive blonde woman called through the window, "Excuse me! Do you know the way to the library?"

Since they'd come in that way, Alex knew exactly where it was. "Head to the stop sign and hang a right."

"Thanks," she said with a blush. "It's my first day, and I'm already running late."

"New in town?" Alex asked.

She studied his SUV, packed to the brim with belongings. "You too?"

Alex couldn't help but think she was awfully pretty. Awfully pretty and maybe in need of some friends. He grinned, an idea occurring. "Maybe we'll stop by later and check out some books."

"We're offering hot apple cider and storytelling at four."

"Are you now?"

"Can we, Dad?"

"I think we might be able to work that in."

"I'll watch for you…?"

"Alex. And this is Winston."

"Monica." She smiled, and Alex's heart beat faster, like he'd overdone the caffeine. She appeared ready to say something but then thought better of it. "I'd best get going."

"Right."

"You won't forget now?"

Alex felt a wave of heat at his neck and wondered if she was flirting. "We'll be there."

"Reading's good for the boy."

"Yes."

"And for fathers too."

Now he was certain she was.

Alex tried to redirect his thinking to the task at hand, but his memory kept homing in on her awesome smile and that sweet way of talking she'd had about her. Like she was from some place far away. But he wasn't here to meet women, for crying out loud. He'd taken a job as the new town deputy.

As Winston carted his stuff indoors, he met his dad's eyes. "She was pretty."

Alex set down his load and rubbed the back of his neck. "Can't say I noticed."

Winston twisted up his little lips. "Da-ad." He gave an exaggerated sigh. "I wasn't born yesterday."

"No, but sometimes I'd swear you were born twenty-five years ago."

He pulled his boy into a hug and stared out the window at the mountains as they turned blue and purple in the dawn. He and Winston were going to like it here. He just had a feeling. They were going to like being in Blayton a lot.

THE END

Book Extras

Character List
In Order of Appearance/Mention

Elizabeth Jennings—young mother, newspaper editor
Claire Jennings—Elizabeth's fifteen-year-old daughter
Nathan Thorpe—Blayton's sheriff, mid thirties
Mrs. Fenton—deceased owner of old Victorian
Bernie Campbell—Nathan's deputy, late twenties
Janet Campbell—Bernie's wife, cashier
Melody Anne—Belle's daughter, Nathan's niece
Belle—Nathan's sister, Melody's mother, librarian
Martha—Nathan's Administrative Assistant, married to Lex, Joy's mom
Mr. Harris—runs detention at the high school
Pinckney Gale—used to run The Town Gazette
Joy—Martha and Lex's daughter
Perry—Claire's love interest, Dan's nephew
Phantom—Claire's cat
Lex—Martha's husband, Joy's dad, communications worker
Dan—Perry's uncle, runs orchard
Penelope—Melody's friend
Lilly—Melody's friend
Jerry—Elizabeth's boss in Richmond
Betsy Jean—Elizabeth's best friend from high school
Phil—Betsy Jean's husband
Cash—Elizabeth's ex-husband
Mrs. Carole—teacher at high school
Mrs. Peabody—Algebra teacher

Parker Family—Trio that disappeared on Halloween night

The Bailey Boys—three brothers in middle school

Character Names
Selected for Significance

Nathan Thorpe—gift from God + from the village
Elizabeth—consecrated to God
Claire—clear
Bernie—brave as a bear
Martha—lady
Joy—jewel, delight
Belle—beautiful
Melody Anne—melody + prayer
Perry—rock
Fenton—from the farm
Phantom—spirit, ghost

* *The Character Naming Sourcebook, Writer's Digest Books, Cincinnati, OH 1994*

The Story Behind the Story
The Ghost Next Door

From July 3, 2103 Blog Post

With the first days of summer upon us, you may not be thinking about autumn leaves and Halloween ghost stories, but I am. I'm deeply into a new tale. Something that's a little bit different but which offers traditional Ginny Baird romanticism just the same. If you've read me already, you know I'm a big believer in happy endings. For it really can't be a *romance* if the guy doesn't get the girl—or vice versa!

When I began this new story, I had originally intended it as Book 4 in my Summer Grooms Series, but these characters and this plot had a whole different direction in mind. Some years ago, I lived in a tiny Virginia town. It was so small, in fact, it was technically considered a village. Life there was cozy and the scenery bucolic, but the feel was a tad isolating, with very few shops and even fewer modern conveniences available.

Far at the edge of this burg and snuggled up against the Blue Ridge Mountains sat a lonely graveyard. I was surprised to see a brand-new house going in across the way and wondered who might choose to live there with such a view in store. Apart from facing rows of tombstones, the new home sat beside a run-down Victorian, the sort of place that could look awfully spooky under a full moon.

The possibilities intrigued me, and I wanted to set a story in this new house. So when I began my current project, that's where I started: with location. Next, I envisioned a young single mom and her teenage daughter moving there from a larger city. They might have relocated quickly and selected a temporary housing solution, not realizing the full implications of the landscape based on the real estate listing they'd reviewed.

But maybe life in this new town isn't really so bad. They're welcomed by a small-town sheriff with gorgeous hazel eyes and a nice, solid build that single mom Elizabeth can't help but notice. When he smiles, her world goes off-kilter and all thoughts of ghostly happenings are set aside. Yet something spooky *is* going on at the house next door. At least Elizabeth and her daughter are starting to think so. In a town where everybody is connected to everybody somehow, it's often hard to draw the line between fact and gossipy fiction.

The story is populated by a rich cast of characters, all in search of their own goals. And while the world and its mysteries swirl around them, more than one couple finds themselves unexpectedly falling in love. For autumn is a season of change, representing the end of summer and the ushering in of darker days. Though when you find the right person holding your hand, perhaps facing the cold isn't so scary after all.

Look for my new ghost story in August 2013!

With best wishes for spooky endings,

Ginny

A Note from the Author

Thanks for reading *The Ghost Next Door (A Love Story)*. I hope you enjoyed it. If you did, please help other people find this book.

1. This book is lendable, so loan it to a friend who you think might like it so that she (or he) can discover me, too.

2. Help other people find this book: write a review.

3. Sign up for my newsletter so that that you can learn about the next book as soon as it's available. Write to GinnyBairdRomance@gmail.com with "newsletter" in the subject heading.

4. Come like my Facebook page: http://www.facebook.com/GinnyBairdRomance.

5. Comment on my blog: The Story Behind the Story at http://www.goodreads.com.

6. Visit my website: http://www.ginnybairdromance.com for details on other books available at multiple outlets now.

Printed in Great
Britain
by Amazon